DEFEND THE MIRAGE

A STORY OF REDEMPTION

J.K. JONES

INDEPENDENTLY PUBLISHED

A STORY OF REDEMPTION

Defend the Mirage

Disclaimer

ISBN:978-1-998809-17-2

Print: Independently published

Cover design by: J.K. Jones

Contents

CHAPTER 1

BEAU BLACKWELL

BEAU BITES HIS LIP until he draws blood, lowering his face deeper into the mud. A murky sky spans out above him, endless and vast. It's sometime before dusk. The shadows in the grass grow, and the light fades beyond the horizon.

"So good, so *tight*," Larry whispers in his ear.

But Beau's already gone. Soaring from this world and onto the next. Thoughts of the past consumed him. He tries not to go there, tries not to think too passionately about Richard and how, in the end, everything came crashing down around them.

Even crawling around the pits of hell, Beau can still see his eyes: wide, crystal blue, like sapphires glowing in the dark. He can still feel the everlasting kindness that brought Beau from the brink of despair.

Creed wants to be on the road. Away from civilization, away from prying eyes.

Everything from the past is wiped clean until only the whore, and the junkie remains.

They move from town to town, from motel to motel, until they eventually forgo them altogether and hide in the forest, off the grid. Creed says the cops can't track them there.

On the road, they meet guys, wicked men on the run, just like they are. They huddle together, whispering about a nearby warehouse, housing guns and money from the cartels.

They set up camp. Beau makes sure to keep his distance. It doesn't last very long. Creed makes a deal, a high for a fuck. A fair trade. One that he doesn't even blink at.

Larry comes to him, pot belly and stinking of piss and shit.

The second Creed and a few other men leave camp, Beau is thrown onto his stomach, pants wrenched from his waist, and fucked vigorously raw.

Larry is panting above him, wheezing in his ear like some dying chinchilla. He thrusts his cock in and out of Beau's hole, the burned and tender flesh making it unpleasant and nearly unbearable.

Through it all, Beau says nothing.

He learned not to make a sound long ago, especially when men are grunting on top of him. The noises and faces Larry make are monstrous, groaning and laboring like some half-possessed demon.

He lets his mind wander and watches the ants scurry around him, and the worms dig into the earth. Nature truly is a beautiful thing, and perhaps someday, he'll start enjoying this rustic life.

When Larry comes hard, he's wailing like a rabid buffoon. It's all so tedious, and Beau stopped getting off years ago.

Voices drift toward him, and Beau quickly stands, pulls up his pants, and sits near the fire. Creed stomps out of the forest with his latest kill slung over his shoulders. The rest of the guys speak rapidly, probably excited to roast the dead rabbits and squirrels.

Larry is already limping away, heading toward the trees to take a piss or whatever the hell he does after they've fucked.

"Wooyeehh!" Creed holds up several critters in his hand. "We're eating good tonight, boys."

They shout their praises, laughing and sharing liquor around the fire. Creed skins the cottontails and roasts them.

Nobody says anything about his black eye or split lip or the way he barely eats. They say nothing when Larry grabs his arm roughly or pats his ass when Creed is absent. The guys never comment when Larry nearly strangles him to death for daring to deny him sexual favors. Of course, they are blind when Beau can barely walk straight the following day, but they continue to bust his ass for not keeping up with the group.

No, Creed wouldn't notice anything like that.

Beau does what he's told and doesn't complain. As he's skinning one of the squirrels, he feels eyes on him. He doesn't need to look up to know exactly who they belong to—Neil.

The bastard is new to their group. Creed found him a few days ago, and ever since, the guy has done nothing but watch Beau. Neil stays away from the men most days, lingering in the back, smoking cigars.

At first, Beau thought nothing of Neil. He is just a random hick like the rest of them. When Neil's gaze began to follow him, it unsettle him.

Those capricious auburn eyes are too inquisitive, too wide, too threatening, hiding a terrifying malevolence. Neil's feral grin, salt-and-pepper hair, and ivory skin do nothing to quell his growing panic.

But what's the point of getting worked up over it?

Beau focuses on skinning the squirrel, studiously ignoring the auburn gaze on him. Blood stains his hands, and the smell of cooking food overpowers the stench of rotting flesh.

The evening light blends and wanes, ultimately settling into darkness. Beau stares at the fire as the embers flicker and slowly die.

CHAPTER 2

WHATEVER THIS IS, IT needs to stop.

They often share looks, brief and strident but so profound and meaningful that Beau is forced to look away. Neil barely utters a word, but when he does, a stillness settles over the group.

Creed doesn't like him. He told Beau, but it's evident in how he treats Neil. He spits tobacco at his feet and openly sneers at him over minor things. The men are beginning to notice the tension.

In answer, Neil only grinds his teeth and tightens his fingers around his gun. That grin, however, remains in place, unnaturally, as if a thunderstorm could come through, and he'd still be smiling.

The months slide into fall. Beau loves this time of year. The forest is gilded with golden leaves yet to fall, a gift to the eyes, and he can almost let this moment of bliss extend as much as the light is spreading over the horizon.

Sometimes, when he lies face down in the dirt with Larry thrusting wildly on top of him, he imagines his old life. He will visualize the soft feathery kisses in the morning or ice cream at midnight. Those memories are buried deep, pushed way down for when Beau can scarcely stand this life anymore.

Today is damp and aromatic with evergreens and mint leaves, a cool colliding mixture of cloudy and dank. Beau takes off at dawn, eager to get away from the stench of the men. The walk through the wilderness is peaceful, with a gentle fog hovering over the forest floor.

A twig snaps, and his stomach clenches. He doesn't need to turn around to know who's behind him. The few precious moments of tranquility vanish, and he spins around, his hands trembling.

"If you wanted some time alone, you should have said so."

Beau gave up speaking long ago. Now he communicates through grunts and shrugs. Besides, it's not like anyone cares what he has to say, anyway.

"Let's get to it," Larry spits. "C'mon, boy, I ain't got all day."

Beau knows that he should obey. Larry outweighs him by tens of pounds and, when he chooses, he can be a powerful adversary. In the beginning, Beau fought a lot, kicked and punched his way through, but Larry always got the upper hand.

Beau doesn't want to have sex—not today, maybe not ever.

Besides, it's never enjoyable with Larry. Most times, it's nauseating.

Larry takes a threatening step forward. "On your knees, boy."

Now isn't a good time to be brave. Beau knows he can't win. He knows that if he loses, things will become infinitely worse for him.

He briefly considers submitting. He contemplates getting down on his knees and opening his mouth wide for Larry's filthy cock.

His stomach roils.

When will it end? The only time he felt momentary reprieve was when he was with Richard.

Beau feels his chest hollow at the thought of his lover long gone.

"Don't make this harder on yourself," Larry grunts. "Get on your fucking knees."

There's nothing left. Nothing to fight for.

The crushing weight of hopelessness consumes him again, and for a while, Beau stands there with unseeing eyes. This wasteland that he inhabits makes him feel gaunt, and exhaustion settles into his bones.

The stillness of the forest that used to call to him now surrounds him like a grotesque cage, a wilderness of carnage and pain he can never escape. A memory flashes before his eyes.

Those precious nights, gazing at the stars; the vows of everlasting love and devotion, of freedom and passion.

For that memory alone, Beau juts his chin out, digging his heels firmly into the earth. "No."

"What did you say, boy?" Larry demands.

"I said no," Beau repeats loudly. "Go fuck yourself! I ain't your bitch no more."

"Well, I'll be a monkey's uncle." Larry sneers. "The bitch has claws? Wasn't it only last week when I fucked that sweet ass into the dirt?"

Beau remains silent.

"Goddamn Blackwells," Larry mutters, striding forward. "Y'all ain't nothing but shit."

Larry punches him in the gut. Beau staggers, panting, but he quickly rights himself and headbutts Larry.

A sickening crunch echoes through the forest, and Larry cries out, clutching his nose. Blood seeps through his fingers.

Beau balls his fists, ready to charge forward. He can kill the bastard now while he is weakened. A hand grips his arm.

"What in the holy hell is going on around here?" Neil demands.

"Get out of here," Larry growls, clutching his nose. "This ain't none of your concern."

Neil fixes his hard gaze onto Larry, and then grins. "I highly doubt that, but I can have you deep-throat my knife. Would you like that, you cock sucking piece of shit?"

"Fuck you," Larry snaps.

"Fuck me." Neil laughs. "Oh, you wish. I'm sure Creed wouldn't take too kindly to someone in his ranks fucking his younger brother."

"Who do you think I made the deal with?"

Neil's jaw works. "Well, it ends now."

Larry glares at him and then spits blood on the ground. "This isn't over."

"This is so beyond over." Neil smirks. "Sometimes life is like toilet paper. You're either on a roll or taking shit from some asshole. That asshole is me. Now, I am going to give you two options. One, you can try and fuck with Beau again, but I guarantee that you'll be deep-throating my knife before you can get near him. Two, you can back the fuck off and crawl back into that hole you came out of. There is no third option. If you so much as glance at Beau... well,"—Neil waves with his knife—"let's not go there, shall we?"

Larry scurries off with the threat of vengeance burning in his eyes.

A long moment of silence stretches between them. Neil dusts off his jacket, then slides his knife back into the sheath wrapped around his ankle.

"Why'd you do that?" Beau asks. His whole body is throbbing with pain and pulsating rage.

"Who else will?" Neil shrugs and walks away, whistling.

CHAPTER 3

EVENTUALLY, BLOOD WILL FLOW.

Creed stole money from the cartels, nearly half a million dollars, more than he's ever seen in his life.

And Creed shared none of it.

The men grow mutinous, their gazes lingering on Creed as if they want to stab him in the back for his betrayal. They barely escape with their lives, and Creed takes the money, disappears with Beau, and comes back when it is all well-hidden.

There are more men now, seemingly crawling out of the depths of hell, aching and eager to join their group of bandits. They want to attack the cartels and take what's rightfully theirs.

Creed welcomes them with open arms, barking orders and making it known he's the leader. They quickly fall in line, doing most of the hunting and scavenging. However, they are easily corrupted.

Beau is walking one day when he sees them.

Five men that joined their group are crowded around Neil, most of them in various states of sitting and kneeling. The whole picture looks strange, almost revenant, and Beau feels like he's intruding on some kind of church service.

Like spiders, they scurry away when he walks by.

He wonders what's brewing between the men. No doubt they are planning a mutiny because Creed pissed everyone off. He isn't even the least bit surprised that Neil is who they choose as a leader.

The man has a natural disposition, standing well over six feet five, towering, a god among incest. Not to mention his lazy drawl, foul tongue, and commanding presence.

The Rebel Brotherhood, he pronounces.

He's vicious, underlying poisonous sadism in his grin. Beau knows all about men like Neil. And he wants nothing to do with them. Hell, he'd grab Creed and run if he had to. It isn't worth losing their lives over something as fleeting as power.

Beau keeps to himself, clinging to Creed more than usual.

None of them cause any trouble, although there is a strange malicious glint in Creed's eyes whenever he gazes at Neil.

Something awful is fermenting between them.

Creed will sneer loudly, spit and throw his weight around like a damn fool. While Neil watches; dark, villainous eyes are observing but never responding.

Of course, the men notice too, and more and more of them are gravitating toward Neil. It is clear what he is doing; Beau recognized it long ago.

Neil is building an army.

Fuck—he can practically see Creed hanging himself with his noose. Shit is going to hit the fan, and whoever is nearby will be splattered with it.

By the time night falls, tensions grow.

Creed suggests that they go out to get some firewood to keep warm. Beau leaves with Creed. When they return, there is pure chaos surrounding the house, and Larry just so happens to be in the eye of the shit storm.

Everything happens so fast.

Neil spits words viciously, circling Larry, the men scream and foam like wolves for blood. Creed is powerless, like an old dog realizing his time is up.

Of course, it ends with Larry's face caved in.

And Neil howling to the moon in victory. It's sick, wrong, so fucking wrong. They murdered Larry in cold blood over a wad of cash they found in his backpack.

This is crazy because everyone knew Larry went out that day. There's no way he'd be able to steal the money in time. Yet they still killed him, his brains plastered all over the floor.

And Beau is elated.

He stares at Neil like he's a god or the devil, wherein this context means the same thing. For years he's hated Larry, imagined his death a thousand times, and now he is free. At that moment, Richard flashes before his eyes; strong jaw, gentle touches, whispers, and promises in the dark. Years have passed, and smiles have faded and waned.

It seems the more he loves the memory, the stronger and stranger it becomes.

Neil approaches him, tossing his arm over his shoulder like they're friends, blood splattered all over his cheek.

"You wanted out. I got you out. You're welcome, kid," Neil saunters off, grinning like a madman.

And Beau beams.

~

IT'S GOT TO be some form of black magic, Beau thinks as he watches the flames dance around Neil's face. The men are strangely complacent, lounging around eating and drinking. It's been six months since they killed Larry and Creed receded into the shadows, allowing Neil to take over as their leader.

The Rebel Brotherhood is born.

The transition was hardly noteworthy since Neil had begun to rally men the moment they joined the group. Hardly anyone even took notice when Creed stopped barking out orders. They're a group of wanderers, nomads, skipping from town to town, with no rules to dictate them, weaving between states.

They roughhouse here and there, but overall don't cause much trouble. Damian and Tanner join their ranks, two men on the run and in desperate need of sanctuary.

Of course, Neil takes them in. They're a bunch of strays, after all.

What strange spell does Neil have them under? What kind of black cloud did he cast over their heads? Beau isn't precisely sure when, but things started to improve under Neil's leadership.

Neil's rule is long and fruitful, and Beau slowly begins to flourish under it. He develops tiers and gives everyone a jacket with Rebel Brotherhood printed on the back. They can find a small city to settle down in, befriend the locals and find employment.

They aren't friends, nor are they enemies, but something strange in between.

~

"I USED TO BE a financial consultant." Neil blows smoke in the air. "I can show you real money."

"What's that?" Beau asks, twirling his cigarette between his thumb and forefinger. It's a quiet night. Most of the men have passed out drunk at the bar.

Neil grins at him. "I used to advise fuckers on how or where to keep their money, investments, and such, but this here," he kicks the duffle bag between them, "is a lot of fucking money."

"Drug money," Beau deadpans.

"I can show you how to clean it, triple it even. Make it ten times what it was before."

"Why?" Beau shrugs. Money is money. It never matters how much he gets; he can never keep it. At least back in the days when he was whoring himself out.

"Commercialization, gentrification, that is the way of the new world," Neil says wistfully. "How long do you think this drug business is going to last? We stay on top for a while. Then another big fish comes to swallow us whole. The old world is fading, a broken system and drug money can only last for so long. Real money, well, that comes from cycling it, from dirty to clean and vice versa."

It makes sense. The cartels are hot on their heels. At least if their money is tied up, they won't know where to look.

"Why did you leave your old life?"

"There was nothing left of it. My son died of stage four cancer. I found my wife dead in the bathroom three days later. They all had the fucking gall to tell me they're in a better place," Neil mutters, taking a long drag. "I hate them. You do too. The hospitals bled me dry for years, treatment after treatment to no avail. We feed into the system; institutions that wring us dry and give us nothing in return. That's why I left. I don't need anything in this world besides my bike and my gun. I became a nomad and never looked back... what about you, kid? What secrets do you have buried under your skin?"

"The deadly kind," Beau says sternly.

"I see..." Neil turns to him. "How long has that knife been in your back pocket?"

Beau keeps a straight face.

Neil asks, "You could have killed Larry at any time... so why didn't you? I could tell you wanted to. Why not?"

Why not indeed?

"You're not weak, kid," Neil continues. "Why pretend you are?"

He's been pretending for so long he doesn't even know the difference anymore. "Mind your own business."

"No... I don't think I will."

Beau is tired. Too tired.

"There's a supplier south of here," Neil continues. "I'm getting too old for this shit. We can triple this in a few months and disappear off the grid. I can show you how, if you're willing to learn."

"And what if I don't want to?"

"You do," Neil replies. "I can see it in your eyes. Restlessness. The men need someone younger. Fresh blood."

Beau considers it and then nods. "Whatever."

Neil chuckles. "Strong roots produce beautiful leaves. Follow my lead, kid. You won't be disappointed."

~

MOST NIGHTS HIS heart tears him apart. The organ is riddled with culpability and shame. He left Richard. He abandoned him.

Beau hates himself for it.

Icy blue orbs stole his breath away. The thick musk of bodies colliding in the night, the touches, kisses, and caresses that drove him mad in the heat of the moment.

He agonized over Richard. For hours and hours, he thinks of nothing else. God—it's so damn painful. The only way to cure this hurt is to turn his heart into stone or rip the organ from his chest.

Either option seems virtually impossible, but there is no way to escape it. There is no way he can outrun himself. Richard is in his veins, in every living cell of his body—ultimately the light of his life, when he yearned for merciful darkness.

Days bleed into weeks, weeks into years, and he starts to find a hollow comfort in the tender memories.

He'll go back.

Come hell or high water.

Chapter 4

Richard Clayson

Four years later...

He jolts awake, mind swimming as his kneecap bursts in agony.

Richard inhales sharply. He fumbles around for his medication; the room is pitch black, not even the moon or stars can penetrate the night. He finds the bottle with pills, choking them down along with a glass of water.

He waits. The pain intensifies, before dissipating. Richard scrubs his face, noting the sweat trickling down his unshaven neck and brow. It's after three in the morning.

Why the fuck is he awake?

A dream.

One of Beau coming to him, with naked lucidity, black hair curled around his eyes, emeralds, and stardust.

Richard cannot resist the sight of him.

Soft flesh encasing brittle bone. Saliva fills his mouth, and he fans the flames of this desire with the thought of capturing that soul. A sweet, impish soul. There is a brightness to Beau that outshines the sun, rendering it feeble in comparison to his magnificence.

To have him would be to capture starlight in silken skin.

On the other hand, so he thought. What was is not what is. Richard understands that. The dream slips through his hands, causing him to chase the remnants of it.

Four years. That's the length of time he's been in the netherworld. Richard recoils.

Bile turns in his stomach. He gets out of bed and limps toward the bathroom. The cane he usually walked with was in the living room and there was no way he was going to get it.

The light flickers as he turns it on. His vision blurs, and the room fades in and out, before coming back into focus. The piece of shit stutters before finally lighting up the room. Richard grips the sink until his knuckles are white.

The pain flares.

It spikes hotly across his vision. When will it end? It won't. Doctors told him it never will. Not unless he could afford a thirty-thousand-dollar knee cartilage surgery. With Lana draining all his pension and what little money he gets from unemployment, he can barely afford himself.

Richard knows he doesn't look human anymore.

They shriek at the sight of him.

The demon has taken form. His mouth is too wide and his spine too long. He does not look tall but rather stretched out in a human ductility. The spacing of his eyes is too far.

He has too much bone and not enough skin. What skin he has is too flawless to pass as natural. His teeth are too sharp and numerous to satisfy human susceptibilities.

Perhaps if it were only one feature so distorted, then he would blend in. However, the culmination of all these features renders him grotesque.

He tried to smile at Kyle once. Of course, his son had stared back completely revolted. Richard doesn't have the muscles anymore to smile. He could only show an enlarged gaping maw of rows upon rows of gleaming sharp teeth.

Richard and the demon have finally become one.

It's not pretty. Then again what is? Richard never cared for looks. He shuts off the light, body aching and soul withered. The bed creaks when he lies down, and the springs dig into his spine.

What kind of life is this?

The life you've chosen, the demon whispers to him. Yes, he did. When he decided stuffing his cock into pretty holes was more important than anything else. More important than family, than friends and love.

Richard closes his eyes.

But finds no rest.

~

"I'M SORRY," Bonnie says, giving him a pitying look. "It's not going through."

The line behind him is long. A queue of growing customers waits for him to hurry the fuck up and pay so that they can get their groceries too.

Declined.

The word flashes on the debit machine as he fumbles for his wallet.

It's the third card they've tried. Richard's face warms, but he's determined to pay for his goddamn food instead of his heading over to the local food bank.

"I can ask Lucina to see if we can waive it again—"

"No," Richard barks. "No, it's okay."

It's not.

But he'd rather pull out all of his teeth than see the fucking haughty expression on Lucina's face. The razor-sharp tilt of her knowing brow and the underlining sadistic gleam. Of course, she thought he deserved this. Probably instructed Lana to bleed him dry and drag him through the mud.

There's no escaping judgment in Byrmonville.

Richard hasn't eaten properly in several days. It must show because Bonnie bites her lip as if she's stopping herself from protesting.

She's a sweet girl.

He wonders if she still tutors Kyle. It's been years since then. Kyle is almost fourteen now, nearly a man. Richard swallows, and then instructs her to put several items back.

Eggs. Bread. Cereal. He doesn't need much.

Bonnie rings him through again and sighs in relief when it clears. She hands him the receipt with a sad smile. "Take care of yourself."

He's surviving. Isn't that enough?

Richard thanks her quietly and limps out of the store. He walks slow, cautious of the wayward cracks in the pavement. He's slipped several times before and nearly broken his back.

He stares at the parking lot, momentarily forgetting where he parked. Shit. Richard groans inwardly.

It's busy today. Richard's hands shake as he looks over his shoulder at the bar across the street. They're a rowdy bunch, brash and thoughtless, shouting above the roar of their bikes.

There is one man that stands out, though.

The Harley rumbles like a bull between his thighs, betwixt treacherous black wheels. The man smirks, cigar hanging low between his rabbit teeth. He talks loudly, giving an unconscious squeeze to the lever on the bike, revving up the engine.

He laughs, a cruel and cutting sound. He's got more ink than skin spread out on a vast muscular canvas. Rumors of their pillaging whisper throughout the sidewalks. A man strides toward them, looking sweaty, and agitated.

Not like the rest of them. This one is different. He's a junkie.

"Do you have anything for me?"

"You've had enough," the man says and turns back to his pack.

No one gets to be the leader of the Rebel Brotherhood without having the morals of a sewer rat. Loyalty can be replaced by savagery and vice versa.

Richard disregards them all.

Choosing solitude above the rancid smell of smoke. He strides languidly with the knowledge that these men are the new infestation in Byrmonville.

Not like the Moonshiners.

Different. Worse perhaps, in their dispositions. Youthful men with a penchant for carnage. Roy will certainly have his hands full.

Then again, why does he care? He's not a cop anymore.

Richard gets in his shitty truck to drive to his shitty apartment.

It's all so lackluster.

With the Georgia heat blazing above, and the sweat pooling on his brow, he wishes things were different.

Then again, only the devil can make changes in hell.

Byrmonville seems to have a large influx of new people. It's not the same small town that he once knew. But a lot can change after four years. The sirens blare across the street.

Richard watches as police cruisers zip past him, their lights flashing hazardously as cars move to the side of the road. He starts the car, his jaw working against the sharp ache in his chest.

Long ago, he used to love that sound.

The thrill went down his entire body as he and Roy gave chase.

The stench of coffee and sweat as they geared up for another bust. Roy's laughter was like wind chimes, his black hair swaying in the wind. *Let's fuck shit up.*

Yeah, let's. Richard would rest his hands on his M1191, feeling the cold steel pressing into his fingertips. For justice, for our children, or whatever other nonsense he would spout.

Richard pulls out of the parking lot, hands clasped tightly on the wheel. What does that matter anyway? When his children hate his guts and justice fucked him six ways until Sunday.

That was then. This is now.

CHAPTER 5

SEVERAL PAST-DUE LETTERS ARE waiting for him at the door.

Bypassing them, Richard puts the groceries on the table. He can only do so much with his leg, so it takes him some time to bend over and pick them up.

The stupid mailbox is broken, so the mailman just stuffs everything under his front door where anyone can see and steal them if they choose to.

He grabs the thickest envelope he can find and opens it. Medical past-due notice. Damn. He shreds the letter. What the fuck is he supposed to do? How can he go back to work unless he attends physical therapy?

How can he attend physical therapy if he doesn't have any fucking money? Richard dumps them all in the trashcan. *Fuck it*.

Who needs physical therapy anyway?

A sharp pain spreads across his kneecap, forcing him to shift his weight. He massages it gently, hissing under his breath.

He's hungry, and tired from the pain and the lack of sleep. His stomach gurgles pitifully as he stares at his bread and eggs. Richard grabs a frying pan and begins preparing his food, thoughts a million miles away.

When it begins to simmer, he goes into the bedroom to take some medication. It eases the twinge in his thigh and kneecap. After he's done, he sits down on the couch, propping his leg against the table.

Richard closes his eyes.

Beau.

The meaning of his existence. His bright soul a beacon crying out desperately for him. The colors in Beau are endless—tangible. There is always some new facet to discover. Beau was always bold and mischievous, shy and rancorous. A vixen.

A traitorous bastard.

His love. His life.

Richard rips his eyes open. Smoke rises from the stove and the smell of burnt eggs wafts in the air. He jumps up quickly, limping as fast as he can to turn it off. The eggs are charred. Ruined.

Shit. He eats them anyway.

Nothing here can go to waste.

~

THINGS ARE not right. Why is it that after four years night is day and day is night? Richard frowns, staring at the coffee pot.

The machine sputters, splattering coffee all over the countertop before whining pitifully. The coffee lands everywhere other than in the actual cup, and by then, he's ready to throw the damn thing in the garbage.

He sighs dejectedly, grabbing the mug and tossing the small amount of coffee into the sink. He glowers at the machine, wanting to smash it into tiny pieces with his foot.

Time ticks slowly in the background, he can faintly hear music from his neighbors across the hall, and the roar of the city life buzzes around him.

PTSD, they said, breathe through it, they said. However, they never told him how the rage would consume him; fill him with fire and brimstone ready to combust at any moment. Richard closes his eyes, allowing the fury to pass as he tries his best to remember his meditation techniques.

They aren't working. Not today. Not the day he needs them to work. He grabs his cane, limping purposefully toward his shitty second-hand couch to grab his medication. He chokes down a few pills, resenting the feeling of calmness as it washes over him. After a few moments of heavy breathing, the fury abides and he feels like himself again.

He checks the time at 12:20 pm.

There's a chance he'll be able to make it for the early bird special still. Richard takes his time, gathering his jacket and wallet. It takes him longer to put on his shoes, his kneecap burning more than usual, the busted cartilage inflamed. Before he leaves the apartment, he catches his reflection in the foyer mirror. His azure eyes look old and tired, his once unruly curly hair is flaccid and oily.

Did you ever love me?

He quickly looks away, walking out of the apartment before the voices can get stronger. Outside is cold, with heavy rain covering the sidewalks. Richard takes his time and ambles along. The possibility of slipping is high, especially with his bad knee and cane.

"Mom! Mom, isn't that Kyle's dad Richard—"

"Shhh," the mother hushes her son quietly. "Keep your voice down!" She grunts at him before gazing up at Richard in disgust. "I thought I told you not to talk to Kyle anymore."

"But he's in my class—"

"Come along." She grabs his arm, forcefully steering them in the opposite direction.

Richard feels hot with embarrassment.

With steady determination, he makes his way over to Greene's Diner. The warmth of the atmosphere engulfs him, and he finds a seat near the back.

Maybelle Armstrong approaches him warily. Her beautiful face is full of pity and sadness. "Hey... how are you doing?" she drawls, offering a kind smile.

Richard forces a smile. "Could be better..."

"Look..." Maybelle rubs the back of her neck. "Daddy says... it's not good for you to come here anymore... bad publicity and all that. You understand, right?"

Richard's stomach plummets.

"I see," Richard mumbles quietly.

Maybelle looks around uncomfortably, her chin-length hair grazing her cheek.

"But... what Daddy doesn't know won't hurt him." She gives him a warm smile. "Just for today. The usual?"

Richard sighs in relief. This is far beyond what he deserves considering everything he's done. He nods quickly, and she disappears into the kitchen.

A few minutes pass before she comes back with his food—grits, and eggs—with a steaming cup of coffee. Maybelle chats with him between orders. She shares news of her siblings and her father, Monroe Armstrong.

CHAPTER 6

THE LUNCH RUSH COMES in, and suddenly Maybelle is swamped with customers. Richard smiles fondly at her hasty goodbye and finishes his food in peace.

It's raining heavily by the time he leaves the dinner. People fill the streets, doing some last-minute shopping before they close for the holidays. He makes it back to his apartment, feeling the cold seep into his bones—at 1:30 pm. Richard picks up his phone, and his hands shake as he dials the familiar number. His grip is tight on the receiver as he waits for someone to pick him up.

"Hello?"

"Lana?"

"Yes."

Richard sighs happily. "T-thank you for picking up. How are you? How are the kids?"

"Fine."

Richard senses the tension in her voice, but he powers through anyway. "Listen... I'm thinking of stopping by tonight. I got some things for the kids, and it's been a few months since I've seen them." His eyes swing over to the Christmas gifts he bought months ago, wrapped neatly in a plastic bag.

Silence greets him on the other end.

"Now, don't be that way. I thought we agreed that—"

"It isn't a good time."

"Lana—"

"I said when the kids are ready. Kyle is still made fun of at school. Ida is too young to understand what's happening... I mean—*Jesus Christ*—Richard, I can barely get a job as it is."

His heart squeezes. All because of you.

"Don't take them away, Lana, please. They're all I have left."

"I would never. You know I wouldn't."

You would, he wants to scream. Instead, he allows her to finish.

"But it isn't a good time. They don't want to see you... I don't want to see you."

"I understand," he mumbles. "Take care of yourself, and let me know if you need anything."

"Roy will take care of it." Yes, how could he forget her new boyfriend, who also happens to be his ex-best friend?

"Okay."

"Goodnight."

She hangs up before he can reply. Richard stands there with the phone in his hand for several moments. Then he crushes the receiver in his fist.

~

LANA PROMISED she wouldn't.

She did anyway. Richard stares dejectedly at the walls. His mind racing with thoughts and promises while he was stuck in hell.

Those are your kids, of course, I would never take them away from you. Behind the glass wall in prison, the promises were sweet nectar, something to encase in his brittle hands.

Lana visited as much as she could. Until she couldn't anymore.

The sight of him behind bars filled her with revulsion. *The kids don't want to see you like that. I don't want to see you like that.* Then she left and never came back. Lana did call periodically. Allow him to speak to Kyle and Ida, but only for short, fleeting moments.

Then he was attacked. His kneecap shattered, and he was stuck in a coma for six months. Richard fell into a deep depression. It was so bad he forgot to put the baby safety gate near the stairs and Ida fell injuring her right leg. The wound was superficial but Lana took it hard and suggested he get better first before having the kids visit.

Once the divorce was finalized, he barely saw them. When he did see them, she always fluttered about with her nervous feathers, as if he could infect them just by being nearby.

She didn't talk about his sexuality. None of them do. Roy made it a habit to never speak about it ever again. Richard finds it so frustrating.

Will they ever see him as what he is? A gay man. Finally able to live in the right skin. Lana pretends that aspect of him doesn't exist. She carries on with life as if her husband isn't queer.

She sweeps it under the rug, and Richard lets her.

Richard doesn't drink. He can't. The doctors told him mixing alcohol with medication would be fatal. So, he sits in silence. Listening to the bustle of Byrmonville, the willow city in the Deep South.

It's nothing like what it was.

Richard feels confused most days. The town grew, exponentially. While the locals retreated, a new breed of foreigners came through.

Technology changed, things transformed, and Richard has been left treading waters of the past. He stares at his worn-down couch; it's orange and ugly, filthy with grime and shit. Richard got it at Goodwill at a decent price months ago.

Lana had taken one look at it and quickly packed up Ida and Kyle, citing a last-minute appointment. Richard feels sick with longing.

Heart encased in a black cage.

The sky darkens, and he drifts off into space. Where Beau is covered in stardust. His arms outstretched, lips red and rosy, begging to be touched and fucked.

Christ—he should hate him.

And he does, viciously. Richard often wants to peel the skin off his bones and pull out each vein with his teeth. Beau played him, used him, and abandoned him.

If only he could turn his heart to stone.

A soft knock brings him back to the present. Richard looks out the window, noticing the darkening sky and threatening clouds.

There is only one person who visits him.

Richard grits his teeth, hands clenched tightly. Is it that time already? He swallows and then gets off the couch with great reluctance. He opens the front door, frown deepening on his face.

"Richard."

Roy looks different. His hair is long and wavy, nearly touching the nape of his neck. The police uniform stretches across an impressive stance of muscles, tight and rippling.

His aviator sunglasses are large mirrors, reflecting Richard's sorrow to him.

"Did Lana send you?" Richard grunts. He knows the drill. He'll call Lana and beg, then, she'll send Roy over to check on him.

It's tiresome.

Old. Richard just wants to see his children. He's missed too much of their lives already. Ida isn't even a baby anymore. She's nearly six years old and barely recognizes him.

It stings.

"No." Roy takes off his glasses. He looks worn, exhausted. "May I come in?"

Richard steps aside, allowing Roy to bypass him. After the door is closed, Richard stands in front of him, waiting. His kneecap aches. It pulsates and throbs, but he'll be damned if he grabs his cane in front of Roy.

The rat bastard who's been his only friend for almost thirty years.

Roy. Who took his wife and children, who was the only person that visited him in prison for four years, that same man that never looks at him with anything other than pity.

Richard can't stand the sight of him yet knows he would be nothing without him.

Roy takes out his wallet, puts some money on the table, and leaves it there. "It's not much, I know it's not even half of what Lana is asking for, but it's the best I can do."

Richard wants to spit fire at him. "I'm not taking your fucking money."

Roy remains silent.

They play this game at least twice a month. He'll drop by with money or groceries; Richard will put up a vicious fight but takes it all anyway.

It's humiliating.

"Shut up." Roy rolls his eyes, then goes to sit on the couch, and puts his feet on the coffee table as if he owns the place.

Fucker.

Richard limps toward the couch and sits down. He nearly sighs in relief when the weight is taken off his knee. "What do you want?"

"I don't know how to say this."

"Just spit it out," Richard grumbles, combing a hand through his wild curls.

It's serious. Very serious.

Richard knows *that* look. It's one they both used to wear when delivering bad news to pedestrians. He braces himself, hands curled like fists waiting for the anvil to drop.

"Casey is dead."

CHAPTER 7

It's been years since he's been back here.

Everything has changed drastically. The walls are a dull white, not like the vibrant yellowish hues they once were. People are bustling around like headless chickens.

Roy leads them straight through, nodding to several of his coworkers as he strides into his office. Richard is apprehensive. He keeps his head down and his baseball cap low.

Luckily, everyone is too busy to notice their old boss amongst them. The laughing stock of Byrmonville. He swallows it, but it doesn't stop the self-hatred from rising. They reach the south entrance, near the psychology department on the first floor.

There is yellow tape everywhere, forensic scientists are taking pictures and walking in and out of the room. Roy lets himself in, then holds up the tape for Richard. "It's not pretty."

What murder scene is? Richard gazes around. His sharp eyes pick up the spatter of blood on the walls and floor.

She's there in the middle of the room.

Eyes wide, throat slashed with a thousand gruesome cuts all over her body. It's barbaric. She had been a withering flower all her days, a rotting seed that grew demented and deformed. He's never liked Casey. Her corrupt spirit made his time with Beau riddled with frantic anxiety.

He rued the day she fired him.

All haughty and righteous, as if her slate was spotless and she didn't spend half of her life manipulating the law by sheltering her son from rape charges. Sick. Wrong.

Richard doesn't feel a thing.

Casey's short hair has grown. Gone are the jagged edges, in its place wispy frail strains of red and gray. The lines within her face have deepened, craved like granite.

The knife cuts make her nearly unrecognizable. The tiny slits are bursting, bled profusely. She must have been alive for the whole thing.

Then the last cut, a slash at her throat. Mercy, Richard thinks.

Richard limps around, careful not to disturb any evidence. He notices the splash of paint on the tiles, then looks up at the wall.

"You're all guilty" is written in large bold letters. The handwriting is sloppy, and illegible, almost as if a child wrote it. Richard notes the footprints on the ground, clunky, and heavy, almost as if this person wears steel toes.

"Her son?"

Roy shakes his head. "He was at the bar last night causing a raucous. I reckoned he may have come here afterward, but Maybelle is adamant he spent the night slumped over the toilet at her place."

"Maybelle?" Richard asks with a frown. "What's Maybelle doing with Damian?"

"Lord knows," Roy replies. "Long story short, he's got a tight alibi and seemed beyond distraught that his mother was dead. He's damn near inconsolable."

Richard nods heavily, then leans closer to Casey's dead body. The cuts were too precise. The blade must have been sharp and clean as if the perpetrator knew exactly what he was doing.

"No gag?" Richard asks, looking at the skin around her mouth.

"That's just it," Roy responds. "No gag, nothing to block her from screaming. Either she knew her attacker, or she was expecting it because nobody heard a sound."

"Check the vents," Richard says. "Maybe they put a sound blocker in there."

Roy swears, then orders the nearest officer to have the whole area checked completely. Richard continues to walk around the body, and he takes mental notes here and there about her position, the skin torn under her fingernails. "Where's her shoe?"

"In the back." Roy points to the corridor. "We reckoned she may have been dragged."

Richard nods, looking between the corridor and then back at the chair. "No wonder there were no screams," he mutters to himself. "What type of object do you reckon?"

Roy thinks for a moment. "Mm, thick, blunt. I'd say a crowbar or wrench."

"The person must have knocked her unconscious and then dragged her to the chair, then proceeded to cut her to shreds."

Roy's eyes widen. "*Fuck.*"

"Yeah," Richard replies, then walks around the area again. "She was alive but unconscious, so she couldn't scream. The last cut, the one to her throat, must have been when she woke up."

"Jesus," Roy curses. "Who the fuck would do something like that?"

Someone with nothing to lose, Richard thinks, then carries on examining the body. It's strange that she died this way. It is too specific, too calculated. Almost as if the killer wants them to know he did it.

"Any leads?"

"A few," Roy replies. "Some you might recognize. Nothing substantial."

They lock eyes.

A new gang in town. Richard recalls the strong stench of petrol fumes and waves of heat coming off their engines. They usually sit astride a Harley, relishing the deep rumble between their meaty thighs.

Richard watched them from afar. They lurk in front of Avery's old bar, drinking beers and talking loudly. Disrupting the peace of Byrmonville.

Rebel Brotherhood. Not like the Moonshiners. They're different. Better, perhaps? Younger. Not at all like the hardened drug trafficking criminals like Enos and Avery.

They drink, they smoke, and they fuck. Riotous youth with nothing better to do.

Not seasoned killers slicing up people in the social services department.

Then again, stranger things have happened.

~

AFTER SEVERAL hours, Richard's knee began to throb, and Roy notices the telltale signs of him favoring his right leg over his left. "Let's go to my office."

Richard grits his teeth but follows Roy down the corridor toward his old office. The room has been revamped, pictures of his diploma and his accomplishments have all been replaced. Roy took the liberty of placing his pictures on his desk, some of Lana and the kids, a few with Isaac and Houston, and several other guys on the force.

Richard doesn't comment on it.

If he did, he might drive his fist straight through Roy's smug face. They sit across from each other; Roy grabs a folder and reads over it carefully before setting it down.

"Why am I here?" Richard asks.

The question burns on his tongue. Roy came to him earlier that day, itchy and bursting with news of Casey's death at the precinct.

"I need help." Roy gazes at him, hands clasped together tightly. "I need someone I can trust."

"I'm not a cop anymore," Richard says. The words are punched out of him, making his chest ache with overwhelming sadness. "I can't help you."

"Not officially," Roy responds. "I could use some advice on the case. This—it hits too close to home, and if there's anyone that can help, I know it's you."

Richard doesn't like this game. He fucking hates it.

"Get to the fucking point."

Roy's eyes darken, the blackness bleeds into the pupils. A shadow of the monster before. The man that tore apart his life, exposed Richard by tearing him to shreds in front of his colleagues.

Richard Clayson isn't a fag. I've been his best friend for thirty years.

Richard gazes back, jaw clenched tightly. They aren't friends. He wants nothing more than to reach across the table and strangle Roy with his bare hands.

"Fine." There he is. "I'll cut the shit. Casey was looking to reopen the case against Beau. That's why I called you here. She wasn't just digging; she was trying to get an indictment for Blackwell... did you know about it?"

Richard feels like he's been doused with ice water.

Impossible. He bows; his breath feeling like it was being stamped through his lungs. What in the hell possessed her to do that?

Richard can't handle it. The room is caving in. Walls shrink and screech, their voices wailing of the injustice in the past. His hand thickens, claws elongate into sharp talons that threaten to tear and shred.

"Calm down." Roy is suddenly crouched beside him, touching his shoulder. The warmth bleeds through the fabric on his shirt.

Richard jerks away, head-spinning wildly as he comes back to himself. He reins the demon in tightly. "An indictment?" he repeats the poisonous word.

"For you and Beau."

CHAPTER 8

CASEY HAS ALWAYS BEEN vicious. She saw a wound and decided to tear it open with her tongue and teeth. Richard is glad she's dead.

For her secrets are buried with her.

Richard leaves the precinct, his heart heavy as lumber. He makes it to his sham apartment, crushing the door handle just to get out of the car.

Justice. Ha! What kind of justice is this?

Richard did four years for his crimes against Mason. Manslaughter they said. As if it wasn't at all premeditated. Richard meant to kill the bastard, and he'd do it all over again.

As for obstructing justice, evidence tampering, witness collusion, Richard pleads the fifth. It's all water under the bridge, he thought.

What did Casey gain from drudging in muddy waters? Why try to drag Beau back? Leave him be. Richard wrenches open his front door, bursting with rage.

Roy had given him the folder. "Keep this between us."

The snake asking the grasshopper for trust.

Richard had snatched it quickly and left. This is what Casey had been looking into. The file was big, thicker than most.

Names, places, addresses. His stomach roils. This is it. Richard dumps the folder on the table, thoughts racing as he stumbles around his apartment.

He doesn't look at it.

If he does, he'll lunge and read through each page as if they are a lifeline. If Casey was working on an indictment, that means she knew exactly where Beau is.

Richard laughs bitterly. The horrid sound spills from his mouth as tears fall from his eyes. Beau doesn't want to be found. Not now and not ever. For years, Richard never understood why.

His last words cut straight down his spine. *I've never loved you.*

Of course not. Why would he? Richard, the exasperating fool that he is, thought differently. For his love had been an unrequited, one-sided devilish coin that deceived him.

Beau would never forget the wicked lust that was inflicted upon him. That he had been deprived of his childhood thrice by a maniac.

No. Richard will never look for Beau. Not today, with his heart, ghoulish eyes, and beard, and damn putrefactive body.

The room spins, Richard's hands clench as his lungs threaten to explode. He grabs the folder with all his might and dumps it into the trash. Then he snatches the bag and tosses it outside into the dumpster.

By the time he gets back inside, he's completely wrecked.

His knee throbs ceaselessly, sweat covers his lower brow as he staggers toward the couch. Reliable Richard is sick with longing. It burns across his skin like red fire ants.

Beau is better off wherever he is.

Away from the hell hole that is Byrmonville. The small town is riddled with vampiric men stalking the night.

The past is past. Richard will plunder toward the future.

With his head barely above water.

~

THE BIRDS ARE quiet today.

He can only hear quick, warning warbles between each of them. Perhaps they sense the lingering presence of a demon. After all, they had never caught the demon lurking in Byrmonville. But that is a matter for another day when the sun no longer shines so beautifully.

It would be a shame to ruin such a lovely day.

Richard scrubs his face, then picks at the meager breakfast he prepared. At noon the sunshine fades, giving way to threatening storm clouds in the lowering sky. Richard watches the rain against the window, and it trickles like a torrent.

He can't afford a T.V., so he sits in silence. Alone with his thoughts and the demon that slowly consumes him. At some point, he dozes.

His mind was too restless at night to still even for a moment. It's made him equally exhausted and irritable during the day.

He sleeps for a moment, then jerks awake at the sudden knock on his front door.

Richard grunts. He thumbs his knee and then rises from the couch. What time is it? He checks the clock, after midnight. He frowns, wiping the drool from the corner of his mouth.

Another knock. This time more insistent. Richard gets up slowly. He makes his way toward the kitchen and grabs his gun from one of the drawers.

Never can be too careful. In prison, he learned to have four eyes in the back of his head. He tucks the gun near his spine, covering it with his long shirt. "Who is it?"

No response. More knocking.

Richard steels himself, pulse juddering as he opens the front door.

Maybelle Armstrong stands before him completely drenched.

What the hell? Richard is too shocked for words. Her white shirt is completely drenched, and his eyes dip down to stare at her erect nipples. "Maybelle—"

"Can I come in?" She pushes past him and then closes the front door behind her.

Richard stands there stupefied as she walks around his apartment, picking up trinkets here and there. Something is wrong. He doesn't need to be a cop to know that. "Did something happen? Are you alright?"

He should call Monroe. Despite their falling out over Beau, he can relate to him as a father. If it were Ida, he would expect the same.

Richard swallows, then grabs a blanket from the linen closet. "Here." He thrusts the blanket at her, his eyes averted.

Maybelle doesn't say anything, but she uses the blanket to dry her hair and wraps it around her shivering body.

Once she is covered, Richard sits down gingerly beside her, a deep frown on his face. "What are you doing here? It's late... if you want, I can take you home—"

"Don't," she mutters. "I can't go back there."

Richard sighs.

"Let me at least call Monroe—"

"Richard." She latches onto his arm desperately, eyes wide with fear. "I can't go back there—" She cuts herself off, tears falling down her cheeks. "I'm guilty. I'm guilty."

"Try to calm down." Richard touches her arm gently. "Start from the beginning. What are you guilty of?"

Maybelle shudders, bottom lip trembling as her nails dig into his flesh. It hurts. Richard nearly jerks back but forces himself to remain still.

"I did it."

The demon appears, wraps her up like a dark cloak, encasing her in fog and mist. Lips with razor-sharp teeth enclose around her throat, biting down ruthlessly.

Her eyes shine with a cutting fierceness. And Richard knows before she opens her mouth what she's done. The same malice is reflected in his own eyes.

Justice was served. Defend the innocent, kill the wicked.

Maybelle has done just that. Richard's heart slams against his chest. He stares back at her with wild abandonment.

"I killed Casey."

CHAPTER 9

MAYBELLE DOESN'T SPEAK ANYMORE. Her lips are clamped shut. Richard sits in the stillness, relishes the deep ache in his soul for the loss of innocence.

Maybelle's lips tremble, her tiny hands clenched at her side. Ideally, Richard knows there is no way she killed Casey.

They're similar in weight and height for starters, meaning that it would take her considerable strength to grab Casey and drag her into the chair.

Although Casey worked in the Justice Department, she was still trained and wouldn't be easily overcome. Physiologically it doesn't make sense. Not impossible, just improbable.

Richard's been around long enough to know that.

She didn't kill Casey. Maybe she knows who did.

"Okay," he drawls, then scrubs his face. "How did you kill Casey?"

Maybelle's bottom lips trembles, and her body wracks with sobs. "I don't know! I just know I killed her."

Well... that's helpful. Richard suppresses a deep sigh. Faintly, he can smell alcohol. It wafts into space and sits at the back of his tongue.

She's drunk.

It's startling, this knowledge. Who knew that Maybelle, the resident good girl, would be drinking? Then again, culpability could drive anyone mad.

"He said—he said he liked me," she sputters, hiccupping. "He said we would always be together—then he—I didn't want it—I told him no—"

She shatters before him.

And Richard does his best to gather the wayward pieces in his hands. Maybelle's cries pierce his heart.

He knows what happened.

Damian.

Sandy blond hair, a cool smile, shining blue eyes. Richard remembers the case he read, how each woman was brutally beaten to a pulp before being viciously raped.

Their faces were nearly unrecognizable. Each of his mug shots looks smug, entitled. Head tilted up, blue eyes shining with repentance.

Anger heats like a fireball inside him. *That bastard*. He can't ever stop, can he? How many women have been silenced by Casey? How many women are burdened with the knowledge that they will never get justice?

Casey robbed them of that.

Perhaps, that's what each cut represents. Richard hugs Maybelle tightly, stroking her short brown hair.

He doesn't have the words for comfort. They died long ago, beaten to death by this cruel world. Maybelle is a sweet girl.

Although his thoughts have occasionally been impure, she doesn't deserve this. "Try to calm down," Richard says. "Start from the beginning."

Her tail is an elaborate lie.

Riddled with plot holes the size of canyons.

Maybelle went drinking with Damian. Things got heated; he wouldn't take no for an answer and forced himself on her.

She filed a complaint, ready to press charges, but Casey intervened, threatening lawsuits for defamation and slander. It was too overwhelming, so she dropped the charges.

Then in a fit of madness, she confronted Damian the night of the murder. He got piss drunk and apologized.

Maybelle went to the precinct to tell Casey she was going to reopen the case. Of course, she had been unreasonable, spouting the same threats until Maybelle lost her temper and hit her over the head.

After that, she left.

Richard listens to her sweet lies, flowing like milk and honey. *Suspension of disbelief*, he thinks snidely. It's a nice story.

But years on, the force won't allow him to take it as fact.

The one thing he will take is that Damian molested her. That is irrefutable, but the rest? Questionable indeed. Not to mention, Maybelle's pupils are wide, dilated. They frantically dart about as if she's seeing things that aren't there.

Drugs? Perhaps.

"*What* did you hit her with?"

"I—I don't know, a shovel or something."

Or something.

Richard thinks for a long time. Maybelle may believe that she killed Casey by knocking her out. Blunt trauma to the head, at a precise point, can be deadly, after all.

The public doesn't know the gruesome facts of the murder. Roy has kept most of it from the media. Whatever has been leaked seems to be the head wound and nothing more.

"I'm sorry that happened to you."

"Yeah, well." Maybelle takes a shuddering breath. "Nobody believes me. They all say I wanted it—that I consented because—but I didn't want it—"

This town is full of bloodsucking demons.

Having been one of them, Richard can only offer his soft condolences. "I believe you. Everything you said about Damian."

"Thank you." She gives him a watery smile. "I knew you would. That's why I came here."

Is that why? Richard truly wants to know. He feels undeserving of her confidence. After all, many would say that he was no better than Damian.

Inside he knows they come from the same poisonous roots, taking and taking, but giving nothing in return. "I'm so stressed, between the diner and the grocery store I never get a moment to myself—I can't—I didn't mean to—I just needed it all to go away!"

"Will you confess?" Richard asks.

"Yes," she says softly. "I want to. He shouldn't—" Tears slide down her bloodless cheeks. "Have the power to do that to anyone ever again."

"I'll take you in the morning." Richard stands on shaky legs. Exhaustion peels over him, and he sighs again. "Sleep here tonight."

"Okay," Maybelle says, tucking her hair behind her ears. "Thank you again, Richard."

He nods, then retreats to his bedroom.

That night he dreams of the lagoon. The weight of water on his skin and the weightlessness are soothing combinations. Ponds, lakes, springs—all bodies of water become a refuge.

The clear waters entice the baring of skin. Shameless, Beau spread wide upon the sand. Helpless, Richard watches the display from behind until heat warms his ears.

Paradise.

In his mind, Beau will forever hold the wide-eyed, unsung innocence. A heart-wrenching beauty, with raven hair and emerald eyes.

He lives nowhere else, except in the past.
That is where he dwells tonight.

CHAPTER 10

SHE'S GONE.

Richard knows the moment he gets up. Not that he expected anything less than that. These types of things take time, especially when witnesses have been coerced and beaten into submission.

Whatever Casey threatened her with rocked her to the core. Made her believe her truth wasn't validated. It might be best if she spoke to someone on the force.

Perhaps Tanya will be better to alleviate any of her misconceptions regarding the process. Richard walks into the living room.

The rising sunlight pouring through the ornate and wrought wall panels illuminates every speck of dust dancing in the air.

Blankets are folded neatly on the couch, along with a small note in elegant handwriting. *I'm sorry*, it says. Richard understands. In her own time, she will come forward.

Until then, all he can do is wait.

He picks up the phone, dials Roy's number with grudging practice. It rings several times before he picks up. "Roy Rhett."

"Maybelle confessed."

There is silence on the other line. "Horseshit."

"My thoughts exactly." Richard launches into the story, remembering to be as detailed as possible, even down to the alcohol on her breath.

"Impossible."

"Well... I believe the molestation from Damian happened... that's highly probable... but her hitting Casey with a shovel? Now that's debatable—"

"*Richard,*" Roy clips. "Monroe took Maybelle and his family out of town a few days ago."

Everything grinds to a halt.

Richard blinks rapidly, his eyes taking in more light. Every part of him coils, stomach-churning as the words come crashing down around him.

Vaguely, he recalls the demon's cloak, the swarm of mist and darkness surrounding Maybelle. How her eyes flickered unnaturally luminous, golden flecks with razor-sharp teeth.

This happens sometimes. Dreams. Images. Sometimes they're real, and sometimes they're not. After the war, Richard stopped being able to tell the difference.

Shock comes. Then devastation.

Richard is shaken to the core. Yet, his mind is already in shambles. What is there left to break? The demon kisses his cheek like a lover, then sits down in front of him.

You tricked me. He wants to chuckle. Manically, laughter bubbles in his throat, and it takes everything in him to snuff it out. He thumbs the paper in his hand, trailing his fingers over her neat handwriting.

The note is real.

Richard's frown deepen. His head feels like it might split open. Maybelle was here, drenched to the bone and spilling her guts.

It was real.

Perhaps Monroe told Roy that so he wouldn't ask any questions. After all, he had two daughters he thought were completely pure.

No father would ever want any images of their daughter tainted or shattered.

"Are you still there?" Roy demands impatiently.

Barely. "Sorry. I'm here."

"It couldn't have been Maybelle—"

"I agree," Richard speaks through clenched teeth. "But she was here last night. I saw her."

Roy goes quiet. "Okay, maybe she managed to slip away... I don't know... nothing is making sense... Maybelle couldn't have hurt Casey... we have a suspect in custody already."

His head is underwater. Trying to make sense of what is and what isn't. It makes him doubt if the conversation with Maybelle was real.

Has he lost his sanity? He can't even tell the difference. Richard is sick to his stomach. Everything is wrong. He can't talk anymore. He wants to hang up, crawl into a hole, and die.

"I see... Well... if you don't need my help—"

"It was Damian," Roy plunders through. "He confessed."

~

THE WORLD TILTS upside down.

Richard marvels at it. The earth shifts and sharpens, bending and contorting until he is practically on his head. This seeming impossibility has become utterly and completely possible.

Most murders are carried out by someone close to the victim.

Although Damian had been his first guess, he is still surprised.

Like all the residents of Byrmonville, Casey abandoned Richard, shunning him as one would steaming shit on the sidewalk.

To Richard, it isn't at all believable. Who knows? This might all be some fevered dream. Richard's mind drifts, slipping between the chinks like water.

"I need you—"

"I'm not a cop anymore," Richard says finally. "You shouldn't... that one time was a favor... I can't help you."

That's a lie.

Richard is probably the only person that can. Investigative work was his specialty. During his fifteen-plus years on the force, he solved more cases than naught.

He loved it until it tore a hole in his heart and ripped his family to shreds. Yet, the case is like an itch. One he desperately wants to scratch.

Roy doesn't say anything for a long time.

It's awkward. So very awkward. Roy needs his help, and for the first time, Richard refuses to give it. He can read between the lines, fill in the blank spaces.

I've been there for you, and you can't be there for me. How can he? Richard cannot legally help on any case. It's a huge conflict of interest, no matter how skilled he is at solving them.

It would implicate them both.

Unless Roy is desperate or keeping something else from him.

"I understand... I'll contact Maybelle and see what she said." Roy sighs. "Take care of yourself."

The line goes dead.

CHAPTER 11

THE HARLEY-DAVIDSON SPEAKS GUTTURAL, thunderous retort.

Richard watches as a group of bikers gather at the bar. Their motorcycles crackling, the rumble and roar of the straight pipes, waves of heat coming up from the engines.

He imagines that it's not at all about the destination but the rush of the wind and dust. Being in control of the elements.

The Moonshiners were like that.

Richard recalls Mason's hardened face, the lazy days of sweltering heat with Enos and Avery lounging about near the sidewalk. The smell of fog mixed with slight gasoline fumes, which always seems to ruminate in the air around them.

Gone are the criminals of the past.

Now there are newcomers. People he's never seen before, faces twisted and deformed, more scar tissue than skin. The leader stands several heads taller than the rest, jack-o-lantern smile, copper eyes brimming with masochism and the promise of caressing violence.

Who are these men? They're ruining the pastoral view of Byrmonville.

Rebel Brotherhood. The name is branded on their sleek leather jackets.

"Move out of the way, loser!" a man shouts, zipping right past Richard. It jostles him, and he almost loses his balance as the guy makes his way over to the group of men.

Idiot. Richard nearly sneers, then calms down. From far away, he looks familiar.

It's all déjà vu. Not several years ago, he was in this very spot, talking to a black beauty, smoke curling around his lips and tar spewing from his mouth.

Beau.

Christ—he should have captured him. Held him to his bosom and never let go. But humans do not fare well in captivity.

They warp.

Let me, Richard thinks, achingly aware of the words falling like stones. *I can give you eternity.* He cannot conceive any thought otherwise.

Beau smiles.

There is no mischief in the smile—only sadness. It is the slow unfurling of regret—petal-soft and painfully transient.

To hoard him away like a treasure is no love at all. They both know. Richard would keep him safe and, in doing so, suppress Beau's very character. He would stifle his fairy lover, suffocate him so thoroughly.

That's why he left. To remove Richard's heel on his neck.

Richard pivots sharply, walking with his cane to the grocery store, ignoring the jeers of the biker gang across the street that sound after him. Once he's far away, Richard marinates in the silence, wishing and hoping things are different. Yet, still, all he sees is Beau.

And his everlasting regret.

~

"HERE FOR pick up?" Bonnie chirps, her blonde hair pulled into a frizzy bun.

Richard frowns, his hands tightly gripping his cane.

"Pick up?"

"Yeah." She beams, rushing over to grab several large bags of groceries. "They're pre-ordered for Richard Clayson."

Pre-ordered? He takes them gingerly.

The brown bags are stuffed with cut steak, chicken fritters, vegetables, seasoning, and the works. It's the most food he's had in weeks.

But he only came here to buy milk for his cereal.

"Does it say from who?" Roy most likely.

"Ahh." She looks at the paperwork. "Nope."

The rat bastard. No wonder he hung up so quickly.

"No, thank you."

He gives it all back to her.

Because fuck Roy. He doesn't need his charity.

Just because Richard doesn't want to work on the case doesn't mean he can't buy his own fucking food anymore.

"Wait—" Bonnie sputters. "I can't—I mean, they're already paid for, so I can't return them—it's a full week of groceries here and—don't you need it?"

Of course, he needs it.

However, this food came with a cost. If he accepts it, he knows Roy will come back with a favor.

Something to do with the case.

Richard doesn't want anything to do with him. They aren't friends. He isn't a cop anymore. He's done pretending that his life is worth something.

Bonnie's eyes turn pleading, and she chances a look over her shoulder to make sure nobody is around. "I think you should take it," she says softly. "At least... it should give you peace of mind that there's still some good left in this world."

There isn't. Richard doesn't want to shatter her optimism, though. "Fine, but only because you asked so nicely."

She grins and helps him carry the rest to his car.

He'll dump it all in the trash can next to his complex later. No way in hell he's taking anything from Roy ever again.

Richard would rather starve.

~

"PAID?" Richard exclaims, suspiciously eyeing the six-hundred-dollar bill for his prescription medicine. "In full?"

"Looks like it." The pharmacist gives him a deadpan look, then looks behind him at the growing queue. "It's all here." She shoves six months' worth of pain medication toward him. "Anything else?"

"N-no, I—"

What the fuck? Richard scowls at the large bag. Who did this?

There's no way Roy or Lana would have the funds to pay for this. Nobody besides Monroe would offset the cost, which doesn't make sense because he hasn't spoken to him in years. Maybelle?

But then again, why?

Because she spoke to him one night? Even that he found hard to believe.

"Are you sure this isn't some kind of mistake?"

"Nope," she says, sighing impatiently. "Payment was made by credit card. I can ask Mickey to look into it and then give you a callback."

"Please," Richard says, his chest feeling tight. "I need to know."

"No problem." She smiles, then looks over his shoulder. "Next!"

Strange things are happening.

Richard feels uneasy all the way home. Nothing makes sense anymore. Who would have the funds to buy him groceries? As well as pay for his medication?

Who would gain access to that information? Or even know if he had any outstanding bills? It's all so bizarre.

The last thing he wants to do is call Roy to discuss it. Whoever did this will reveal themselves.

CHAPTER 12

THE DEMON CRADLES BEAU'S face in its bloody hands.

A bloody mouth meets a bloodless mouth. When they part, willing and unwilling, Beau's mouth is red from more than a kiss. A metallic taste lingers on his tongue.

You may call me a monster, but I will always be your monster.

Richard jerks awake. His mind is numb from the nightmare that plagues him nightly. Why must he dream of something so gruesome? He gets dressed to go nowhere and do nothing.

He mostly does it out of routine. Sometimes, if he feels particularly adventurous, he'll go to the park and feed the ducks.

Not today.

Today he longs for solitude. Never-ending silence that seems to stretch on in this hell. It's been a week, and things have gotten even weirder.

Bills have been mysteriously paid.

Garbage missing from his disposal. Richard always struggles to take the large bag out near the back, especially with his knee flaring in pain.

Now it seems he doesn't have to. Everything is already put out for him the next day, including the recycling.

It's fine. Dandy.

Except, it raises the hair at the back of his neck. Of course, he is no stranger to fear. It cloaks him, ubiquitous as sunlight on splintered streets.

Being scared is normal, inescapable, yet he can't help feeling as though this goes beyond that. Someone is watching him, haunting his footsteps.

He knows because his mail ends up in a mysterious box near his door. Not dumped on the floor but stuffed neatly, encased in a beautiful wooden mailbox mounted on the wall.

The drill holes look fresh and sleek, almost as if someone with expert craftmanship did it. Richard finds it all so wonderfully unnerving.

Who is this person trying to make his hell a paradise? Who cares enough to take the time to alleviate the stress of a cripple?

He destroyed himself.

Richard knows he deserves nothing but the town's contempt, but someone somewhere thinks differently. Lately, at night, he hears strange sounds.

The deep roar of a motorcycle, a burst of smoke as it speeds away into the night. Those bikers never stay this far into town.

Richard wipes his forehead. In Georgia, there is nothing timid about the heat. It comes in thick, pulsating waves. The heavy air hangs close around sticky skin and saturates the atmosphere. More often than not, he's lethargic, lazing around behind a large fan.

At lunchtime, he grills some steak.

It's the best food he's had in a long time. Richard smiles as he recalls Lana's cooking. The steak she made was somewhere past well-done and partial cremation. It was so tough he would need a hacksaw to cut through it. Lana used to beam at him, dewy eyes proud and arrogant, urging him to try it and smash all his teeth in the process.

They were happy then.

Richard eats in silence, cutting his food and chewing softly. He thinks of Kyle and Ida. Where are they now? He has no clue.

He's missed the most important parts.

Richard has tried to stop by several times unannounced. Lana doesn't like it and makes sure he leaves as swiftly as he comes. *Roy will handle it*, she says, trying to drive a spear through his heart.

Fuck her and Roy, he thinks bitterly. Once he gets some money together, he'll petition the courts. There is no way she can keep his kids away from him.

It's been weeks. Not even a phone call.

Richard leaves his apartment, unable to quell the overwhelming waves of depression. It curdles in his stomach because deep down, he knows, he deserves it.

Nobody loves a demon.

~

SALTY DROPLETS bead on his temple like summer rain. Down his back is a dark stripe amid the white color of his t-shirt, a spreading map of perspiration.

His hair curls like ringlets on his forehead as he strides toward the diner. Many of the men have forgone shirts entirely, sitting under the shade of the buildings.

Richard steps inside the diner and sighs at the burst of air conditioning that hits his skin. Although he's not welcomed back here, he wants to check on Maybelle.

Just to see if everything is okay.

Maybelle is swamped. Amid the heat, she wears a white long sleeve shirt and tight jeans, taking orders here and there while she bustles around the diner.

"I'll be with you in a minute," she drawls, stilling the moment their eyes lock.

Richard offers her a small smile, then takes a seat in the booth near the front.

Maybelle takes a few orders and then bounces over to his table. She looks younger, hair cropped short and brushing against her pale cheeks. "Thank you," she says it so quietly. "For not calling my daddy."

"I should have," Richard responds honestly. "I don't like keeping secrets."

She gazes at him, brown eyes wide and beseeching. "It's not what you think—I'm not—that type of girl—"

"Of course you aren't," Richard says strongly. What kind of world is this? Where the victims are made to feel guilty and ashamed? It's revolting.

"I—I'll report it, I swear—I just—with the diner and Daddy wanting us to go up north last week... I haven't had time you see and—"

"When you're ready," Richard replies. "I can have Roy reach out to you, or Tanya, whichever you prefer."

Maybelle's eyes glaze over with tears. "T-thank you."

"Hey!" a voice sneers. "Can I get some coffee over here?"

"I'll be with you in a moment," Maybelle shouts over her shoulder. "Sorry, what can I get you? I reckon you'll want the usual?"

"Just coffee for now," Richard says. "Maybe a Danish—"

"Hey, honey," the voice interrupts again. "We've been waiting for almost ten minutes! What kind of service is this?"

Richard bristles, hands curling into fists. Who are these people? He peers over Maybelle's shoulder, catching the distinct leather vests and the stench of motor oil.

CHAPTER 13

THEY AREN'T THE REBEL Brotherhood.

No, these men are from somewhere else. Their skin is oily, caked with sweat and grease. Most of them look middle-aged, with large bellies spilling over the tops of their belts.

Maybelle writes down his order quickly, then flutters off to the men in the booth.

They're rowdy, spewing jeers and cheers. Maybelle takes it all in stride, ignoring their lude jokes and keeping things as professional as possible.

Richard moves closer, hands tight and poised, ready for anything. Even though he isn't a cop anymore, that doesn't mean he'll let these bastards get away with harassing her.

Maybelle's already been through enough.

The diner door is torn open.

In walks a familiar lone figure. With a cigar hanging between his lips, he wears a Cheshire cat grin that seems like it can survive a typhoon. Black eyes, and chestnut brown hair, his vest pulls over his muscular chest, making him look imposing.

The man leers, all rabbit teeth, smelling strongly like booze and cigars.

Maybelle jumps, sprinting toward the door in a wild flurry. "Neil—not tonight—please my daddy—" He forces her out of the way, making a beeline toward the other table.

The men continue with their conversation, heedless of the storm thundering toward them. Neil stands in front of their booth, a smile so wide it almost splits his face.

"I thought I told you never to come back here again," Neil drawls. "It seems the Bandidos don't like to listen."

"Yeah? Who the fuck says we have to listen to you—"

Neil explodes with an upswing hook to the jaw. Blood bursts from the man's mouth, spewing all over the countertop. The table erupts. Each man springs into action, fists flying and clawing at anything they can reach.

Richard is moving before he even registers it. "Call the police!"

Maybelle screams as Richard drags her toward the back. "Stay here!"

Then he's in the fray.

Prying men apart, shouting at the top of his lungs. They aren't listening. Neil is an animal, smashing their faces against the table, with a cool glint of viciousness in his eyes.

He's never seen anything like it.

Except once. In his own.

"Stop—the police are on their way—"

A wayward elbow crashes into the side of his skull, the soft spot high on the temple. Richard reels back. Pain explodes across his vision as he stumbles, twisting his bad kneecap.

His pulse speeds up and he breathes very shallow. *When did you become a sniveling rat?* the demon whispers to him.

Neil looks like a god, beating those men into lumps of meat and bone. It splatters, hot and thick against his cheek. His knuckles are bloodied and raw, but it's that smile.

One Richard knows intimately.

He's always been on the wrong side of the law. Being a cop brought him nothing but anguish. Being in the military brought him nothing but despair.

Anger curls hot and unstoppable in his gut, like a blazing inferno that wants to burn him from the inside out.

He did everything right—he was the model citizen, the perfect husband, the perfect father, the perfect soldier, yet still, God decided to piss all over him. He absorbs the trauma, swallowing the pain, then kicks his way slowly back to the surface.

An unbridle fury releases within.

Richard snaps.

He puts out a stiff left, catching the nearest man in the face. The man grunts. Blood bursts from his nose as his head flies back. He slips to the left, evading the counterblow.

Richard hits him with an uppercut that sends him flying into the nearest table.

Fuck them all. He rages, punching and clawing at anything he can reach. It's amazing. Breathtaking. Sickening crunch of bone shifting and cracking.

A rush, like undercurrents, thrums through him. The demon is crackling. Skin blisters, crunching against bone, breaking apart with each heavy blow.

"Police!" a voice shouts, and soon everyone is running for the door. Roy charges in, with several of the squad behind him.

Neil slithers out the back, the cigar still between his lips. The other men try to run, but they slip and slide on the floor, covered in food and blood.

Richard doesn't move, though.

He stands on shaky legs, panting wildly. Shirt torn to pieces, blood pouring like a waterfall from his mouth. But, for the first time in four years, he feels alive.

Roy looks at him, eyes wide in disbelief.

And Richard smiles back.

~

PAIN FROM the wound blazes up with an intensity unlike ever before.

Richard groans, thumbing his battered knee as the EMS bandages up his hand. His knuckles are torn, and he's got a nasty cut above his eyebrow.

Roy paces back and forth, huffing and puffing like a bull. "What the fuck happened?"

For a moment, he wants to shrug like a petulant child, but he keeps his face neutral as he recounts the events leading up to the brawl.

"Another gang?" Roy asks, eyes widening. "A rival gang? The Bandidos you said?"

"Yeah." Richard dabs the icepack on his temple. "Looks like it might be a turf war."

"Perfect," Roy spits. "That's all I need right now."

Richard doesn't respond.

"There's just too many coincidences. I can't ignore them anymore." Roy sighs, then scrubs his face. "That's it. I'll need to take you in for questioning."

What the fuck?

"For what? I didn't do anything—"

"You're making me do this," Roy glowers. "I don't want to, but I'll be fucking doing it. There are too many coincidences, and I don't like it one bit—"

"You don't think I had something to do with this, do you?" Richard demands, staring at him in disbelief. "You're fucking kidding me—"

"Don't pretend you don't know—"

"Know about what? What the hell are you talking about?"

"Cut the shit, Richard!" Roy snarls, eyes blazing. "This is *all* connected to you, and I want to know why!"

"*What?*"

"Casey is dead! Enos is dead! These are too many flukes, Richard! The bodies are piling up, and all these people had something to do with the case!"

"Enos is dead?" Richard parrots. "How? When?"

Roy scoffs. "I gave you the damn folder. Don't act so fucking surprised. It's all connected to one fucking person, the fucking bane of Byrmonville. The bastard couldn't stay away, not even after all these years."

"The folder?"

The one he threw in the dumpster. The one outlining the case in full-fledged detail. "Don't tell me you didn't read it?" Roy grunts. "That you didn't know Casey ordered the indictment several weeks ago and is now dead because of it."

His head is spinning and threatening to explode. Bile rises from his stomach. It's too much. It's all too much.

"You mean—"

Roy gives him a calculating look before it turns sinister, piercing dark eyes are colossal and monstrous. His next words are meant to slice apart his heart.

"Beau... he's back."

CHAPTER 14

Richard isn't listening.

Words pour over him like a waterfall, drowning him. Roy speaks nonsensical things of conspiracy theories and imaginary slights against him. None of it makes sense. Roy glares at him, words fashioned into a knife, sinking in with cold black eyes.

"Can you believe it? The bastard has the fucking gall to buy Gary's old auto shop!"

Richard shatters.

His muscles lock, bones seizing up in ice as his eyes glaze over. Rising bile threatens to erupt. It's all so wonderfully pathetic.

Beau is back.

He's *been* back and hasn't said a goddamn word. The realization twists so painfully, deep and rancid, until all he can smell are his putrefying organs.

Bills and groceries mysteriously paid for; medication bought six months in advance. A mercy, he thought, riddled with holes and ulterior motives. He wants to laugh so hard or he'll cry.

It's an apology. One that doesn't even begin to cover the hellish nightmare of prison. It's as rank as acres on the edge of a flowerless forest.

Soggy older pastures and bloated wilderness.

Like planting a flower among weeds.

"Richard," Roy says, nostrils flaring. "Look, we talked about it... I can convince Lana into making a deal."

That catches his attention. Lana's been vague for a long time, keeping the kids away under the disguise of being too busy. It's complete bullshit.

"What deal?" He finds his voice, brittle and empty, clogging with emotions.

"You can have supervised visits with the kids... on one condition."

Richard already knows what it is.

That means Beau's been in town longer than he initially thought. Long enough for the lords of the underworld to heed the call, beckoning monsters from the abyss.

"Brother," Roy pleads, like trying to catch a falling man. "Don't—" He swallows. "Don't see him again. Promise me. Promise us. You weren't the same after. We just got you back."

Back? Richard wants to heckle, throw his head back and laugh manically. How can he be back? Richard is still in hell.

Of course, he hates Beau.

Right down to the marrow of his bones. Detests him for his mere existence. Richard was bewitched, besotted so thoroughly it destroyed his sanity.

Beau was right to leave. He should never have come back.

Yet, deep down, he knows that's not the reason. The real reason makes him still, shame encases him and chills his bones.

Roy still looks at him like he'll change.

That he'll stop being gay and finally be the man he was before, the criminal chasing, ass-kicking police officer that ate nails for breakfast and shits iron.

Roy never speaks about it. They never acknowledge it. As far as he's concerned, the "gayness" was only specific to Beau. So, if he eliminates Beau, then Richard will no longer be queer.

It's ridiculous, but he's never done anything to discourage his thinking.

Now Roy is asking him to make a choice.

Fear is a kind of madness; it coils deep within him as he struggles to guard the things he deems as precious. Ida and Kyle are his children. He can't give them up.

Yet, can he forsake his true self again? Live a lie for the sake of his family? Shove his feelings and desires under the rug for the sake of normality?

Richard crumbles. It seems old habits die hard. He's too much of a coward to fight back. The weight of his daddy's words hanging heavy in his mind, and ringing like bells in his ear.

I always knew there was something wrong with you.

They deserve more.

So does Beau.

Richard will not trap him, ensnare him into a den of snakes just for his twisted desire. He wants to be better than that, even if it'll bring him to his knees in agony.

"Okay."

"Don't say it if you don't mean it—"

"I mean it," Richard barks, temper flaring. "I won't see him ever again."

Roy sighs in relief. "Good." Roy touches his shoulder. "You're doing the right thing, brother."

Richard nods.

Roy starts to steer him away, rambling on about family dinners and such. It's all he's ever wanted. To be surrounded by people that love him.

But then he looks back.

Hearing the rumbling of the motorcycle in the distance, the sound of rubber shredding against concrete. Whisps of black hair and tantalizing eyes catch him before speeding off down the street.

~

KNOWLEDGE IS power.

Or so he thought. Instead, all it does is pour gasoline onto a spark of fear in his belly. Decimating all of his inner peace.

His imagination runs rampant.

Everything stuck on replay like a carousel ride. Richard initially wanted to protect Beau from all the horrors of the night. Instead, he ended up becoming one.

Perhaps it meant nothing to him.

Richard recalls wildly pursuing the shadows of Beau's infidelity. Traversing along the caverns of his skin, hoping to catch a whiff or scent, only to chance upon ugly bruises and claw marks from other men, seeking to devour what he thought belonged to him.

After all, for Beau, there's no shortage of wicked men. They huddled around him like vultures over prey, picking and plucking the meat from his bones.

Richard was a fool to think overwise.

He sits in the darkness of his apartment, clenching his hands tightly. What purpose does he have? If he cannot love or his love is refused so thoroughly.

It's clear as day. Beau wants nothing to do with him.

And reliable Richard would never force him. It makes his breath stutter in his chest, eyes brim with unshed tears. All he has is memories and tears, the dutiful husband so deep into the closet he needed to burn everything to the ground to avoid leaving it.

There's a strange scratching noise at the door.

Richard frowns, getting up from the couch. It's late. Well after midnight.

Everything comes to a grinding halt.

Kindness can only stretch so far. Eventually, even a good Samaritan wants to be rewarded. Summer breeze envelopes his neck.

The demon ruffles its feathers, bristling silently.

One glance isn't enough to suffice.

He walks slowly to the door, hands shaking and body threatening to collapse. It's been four years. Yet, how could he forget the beating of his own heart?

Richard opens the door.

Heart in his throat, a demon on his shoulders. Not what he was, but as he is. That ever-moving undulating beast, time, seems to slow down. The door between them dissipates into wisps of darkness that float away and reveal Beau in black and brown leather, those dark eyes lined with even more black, long dark hair flying away from his face.

Richard's ears are filled with the sound of his heartbeat.

Beau.

Black hair nearly shoulder-length, fine strands are woven of space-time and starlight. It curls at the nape and over his brow, swaying softly like prairie grass in the summertime. His cheeks are sharper, chiseled. Gone is the baby fat of his youth.

A leather jacket stretches across broad shoulder blades, buttoned down to a narrow waist. Attraction bursts through him, a sane kind of madness.

The pluck of a cello. So deep and sharp it's like the hum of a low melody, a song that plays on and on. Richard floats, body and soul, his face heating with longing and resentment.

Beau left at age seventeen and has returned at twenty-one.

Chapter 15

The world is cruel and wicked.

No words are spoken between them. Richard holds the door open, a silent invitation that allows his former fairy lover to waltz in.

Beau gazes around, quick and judging. Politely ignoring the scurry of roaches and spiders, dishes piling up at the sink, and the cane resting on the kitchen table.

Richard is too spellbound to speak, his heart thrumming in his chest. He clears his throat, attempting to force words from his lips, but none come.

Beau's mouth is drawn into a thin line, the beauty mark noticeable against the edge of his lips. Then he turns back around. Those almond eyes are gems, gleaming and glittering jewels.

And suddenly, Richard wants to smash his face into the ground.

Rage bursts so hot through him; it erupts like fire in his veins. With each passing moment, it grows exponentially until he can no longer breathe.

"What do you want?"

I've never loved you. Beau's vicious words rang in his ear.

Richard only ever wanted to set Beau free: from Mason, from Enos, from Byrmonville. Why did he come back to his cage?

"You know what I want."

He doesn't. How could he possibly know?

"Yes... well," Richard says bitterly. "I don't have anything left to give."

The words cut right down to the bone. Richard doesn't want these feelings; he doesn't want to be so affected by someone who never cared.

Beau's features twist; he crumples as if standing under immense strain. "*Richard—*"

"Why did you come back here?" he plunders through. "Why can't you stay away?"

"You know why."

It's a tether, a string tying them both together. Richard desperately wants to cut it off. For so many years, he imagined this moment. What he would say or do, how he would cradle Beau in his arms and never let go. Whisper promises of devotion and utter nonsensical things.

What's the point of it now? Beau never called or visited, broke his heart, and fluttered away with the wind. He left Richard, and rightfully so.

"Why are you here?" he grits out. "I won't ask again."

"It's not what you think."

"Enlighten me," Richard drawls.

His knee starts to ache. It ripples up his thigh and hip, intensifying with each breath. He limps toward the table and sits down gingerly.

Beau's face hardens. "Fine." He reaches into his pocket. "I'll get right to it then." He places a joker card on the table.

Richard picks it up, frowning. The word Bandidos is scrawled on the back.

"A turf war," he summarizes, thinking back to his conversation with Roy. More like a warning.

"This one is different," Beau replies. "Unlike any I've ever seen."

"What makes you say that?"

Beau levels him with a look. "Because it's interwoven with most of the people in Byrmonville. Listen, we don't have much time. I need your help to stop this from happening."

"Stop *what* from happening?"

Beau remains quiet, he looks down, and Richard can't help but marvel as his black lashes sweep against his cheek.

"The destruction of Byrmonville."

~

HE SHOULD have known.

After all, trees are not surface deep. Their roots grow for miles upon miles within the soil. Turns out the Moonshiners were only the beginning.

It seems his fairy lover was quite the busy bee over the years.

Richard clenches his jaw so tight it might snap. The lies. All of it. Turns out Enos was telling the truth, and they were wrong.

It's bigger than they ever dreamed.

The human trafficking ring Mason started was just the cusp, the tip of the iceberg. Beau left with Creed to avoid the wars with the cartels only to end up right back where they started.

"The Bandidos are the cartels?" Richard demands.

"Not necessarily," Beau replies. "They have deep connections."

He's only getting half the story. Bits and pieces that don't make much sense but allow him to start drawing a bigger picture.

Creed pisses people off. He does that. It's his nature. But now he's pissed off the wrong people. The Bandidos want their money, and the Rebel Brotherhood has it.

"How much are we talking?"

Beau slants his eyes at him. "Half a million."

"Drug money?" Richard scrubs his face. "Christ, Beau."

"I didn't want anything to do with it," Beau mutters. Like that matters.

"Where is Creed now?"

Beau stiffens. "He's dead."

Good riddance. Richard wants to sneer. What kind of brother turns a blind eye to human trafficking? There's no way Creed didn't know Mason was pimping his brother out.

"And the money?"

"Somewhere safe."

Why not give it over to the leader? Why hoard it somewhere nobody can reach? A headache forms at the base of his skull as questions burn on his tongue.

"Is that why Creed arrived in Byrmonville so quickly?"

Beau nods.

He didn't come because Casey called, but because the bastard was on the run and needed to move from town to town quickly and quietly.

"So let me get this straight," Richard sneers. "Creed took money from the cartels, and they sent the Bandidos once they got a lead on your whereabouts, and now, they want the money back?"

"Yes."

Is that what it takes for Beau to see him? Impending death from the cartels and the Bandidos?

Is his love worth nothing?

"I see."

"Richard," Beau says softly. "I'm trying to do something good for once... I want to prevent this from getting ugly. I reckon it's only a matter of time before it does."

"No, you're trying to walk away with half a million dollars."

Beau doesn't even try to look remorseful.

"Why include me?" Richard snarls. "Why not go to Roy about this? You had no problem doing so in the past."

Beau says nothing.

It irks him. Richard coils tightly, ready to spring at the slightest provocation. Damn Beau for coming here. What the hell does he want? To fuck up his life more than it already is? He promised Roy they wouldn't speak ever again, and he is here breaking that promise.

The destruction of Byrmonville. What does that even mean? Who would go so far as to do that? What did they have to gain?

Richard scowls. "Unless... it's another Mason situation? I reckon multiple people are involved."

Beau looks away guiltily, hands stuffed into his pocket. "Never mind. Forget I said anything—"

"Is it?"

"So what if it is?" Beau says quietly, his shoulders slumping. "I'm nothing. Just a Blackwell, the stain on Byrmonville. The town hooker with nothing to offer but his legs in the air."

"That's not true."

Beau glares at him viciously. "It is true. It's so fucking true that I don't know what else is—"

"I've never thought that."

"And you're the only one," Beau grits out. "The only one to say I am worth something."

You're worth everything.

Tears prick his eyes. "You can't just—" Richard's hand trembles. "You can't drop a bomb like that then fuck off again. I won't—" allow it "—it's not right."

Beau steps forward, hand stretched out but drops it last minute. "No, I won't—leave. I'm here for good. I promise."

A promise is a comfort to a fool.

Unfortunately, when it comes to Beau, Richard is always the latter.

CHAPTER 16

BEAU LEAVES SHORTLY AFTER.

Nothing is resolved. Richard doesn't know what he can do to help. It sounds like another uphill battle, this time against far worse adversaries.

Obviously, there is something else going on, and Richard doesn't know if he has it in him to fight anymore.

Things aren't the same.

Beau is older now, worldly. No longer the mischievous teenager with a cool glint to his eyes and a kink to his brow. They're strangers.

Richard doesn't belong in his world.

After all, who could carve out space for a demon?

~

"HORSESHIT," Roy mutters from across the table.

Richard sighs again, tapping his fingers against the steel table. It's odd to be on the other side. Isaac stands in the background, his massive arms crossed over his chest.

It's humiliating. At least they have the decency to look sorry about it. Roy holds his gaze, his notepad filled with wayward scribbles.

"It's true."

Roy scrubs his face. "And that's all that happened? Nothing else."

"Yes." No.

It's best to keep the conversation on what happened at the diner. There's no point in talking about the incident with Beau, at least not until he's gathered enough information.

"Those bruises look ugly."

They do, but pointing it out is rude. Richard knows his face is battered like someone took a shovel to it.

His knuckles twinge with pain, but he doesn't rise to the jab. Roy's always been a bastard. Why would things ever change?

"So, let me get this straight," he says. "You walked into the diner to check on Maybelle, then Neil walked in shortly after, started a fight with the Bandidos—nearly beat half them to death then slipped out, am I correct?"

"Yes."

"But before that, you started breaking up the fight but ended up with a few bruised knuckles? How do you get broken knuckles from breaking up a fight?"

"I'm confused about that as well," Isaac drawls, stroking his red beard.

Richard shrugs. "I was defending myself."

"By breaking another man's jaw?" Roy asks. "See, shit just isn't adding up."

Richard bristles. "What isn't adding up? Ask Maybelle. I was there to check on her. She said Damian molested her and I believe it. Check his case file—he has tons of accusations against him. Things Casey covered up—"

"Why would she go to you?" Isaac asks. "Maybelle ain't like those other girls. She's smart, educated. Her daddy made sure she got the finest education, and she helps out at the diner regularly. Why not come to Houston? Or Karen?"

"I don't know," Richard replies. "She came to me."

"You said she knew Neil?"

"She called him by name."

"It just... dills my pickle is all..." Roy scratches his head, then turns to Isaac. "Doesn't it just seem bizarre?"

"Sounds downright inconceivable."

Richard knows this game. Interrogate the witness using intimidation. Long ago, he used to play and be good at it.

"When I talked to Maybelle, she didn't know who Neil was and vice versa."

No. Richard heard her call him by name. They know each other, and for whatever reason, she is trying to protect him.

"I see."

"Your stories aren't collaborating."

"What reason would I have to lie about Maybelle? I've known her since she was born, fuck, I was the one who christened her. She's like a daughter to me."

"Is that right?" Roy scoffs.

A boiling fury swells inside of him.

"I'm reading between the lines," Roy sneers. "Beau is back for five minutes, and all hell has broken loose. You get into a fucking brawl at the diner, Casey turns up dead, and now it seems we've got a turf war between two gangs heading our way? It seems the shit storm just got started."

"I'm sick of you fucking accusing me of shit," Richard snarls. "I haven't done anything!"

"We don't know that."

"What else aren't you telling me?" Richard demands.

Roy regards him. "We found the murder weapon, a crowbar that was huddled in the back of the police precinct with Casey's blood on it. DNA test shows that it was wiped down with some kind of cleaning solutions to evade authorities."

"Several eyewitnesses saw Damian get into a fight with his mother at the bar," Isaac chimes in. "Then she left shortly afterward."

"This crowbar was used strategically, maybe by someone who used to be a mechanic or had some trade skills because of the thickness, one wrong swipe, and it would have caved her head in completely. Yet, whoever did it wanted her alive, at least while they were cutting her to pieces."

That's sick. Wrong on every single level.

"You don't think it's Damian," Richard says slowly. "Neither do I."

Roy taps his pen on the table. "I think he has something to do with it, but did he murder his mother and slice her to pieces? No. I don't think so."

"Then you're back at square one."

"Not necessarily," Isaac replies. "We have a web, a chain of events that all lead back to the apex. A single gang. The Rebel Brotherhood arrived in Byrmonville several months ago. Since then, things haven't been peaceful. I think it's another Moonshiner situation, one we can't avoid for too long."

"I agree," Richard responds. "Then divide and conquer, create a list of suspects that are close to the victim, then interrogate them—"

"Are you leading the investigation, or am I?" Roy snaps.

Oh. Right.

"Good idea, boss—I mean, Richard." Isaac laughs. "Fuck, it's hard seeing you on the other side... it's screwing with my head and shit."

Richard nods slowly.

"Let's leave it for today." Roy stands. "I'll contact you if I have more questions."

"Okay." Richard grabs his cane and follows them out the door.

"Don't forget BBQ next Sunday at the house," Roy says.

"I won't."

"Remember our deal," Roy says lowly, eye-piercing. "Don't let me down."

I already have. Richard doesn't say it, but he leaves the precinct with a sour taste in his mouth. Knowing that from now on, he is being watched.

CHAPTER 17

HE SITS IN HIS truck for a long time, drenched and drowned like a wet cat.

Richard swallows down the hysteria. It cuts his throat like jagged shards of glass. Why is this happening? What does it all mean?

Enos. Casey.

What do all of them have in common? He drives away from the police station, hands clenched around the steering wheel.

He can't think straight.

Not when his brain wants to implode. Beau is back. He's fucking here, in the flesh with his beautiful fine bones. Yet, Richard's stomach churns.

Why did he come back? What business does he have here? Why buy Gary's auto shop? To plant roots and grow. *I'm not leaving. I'm here for good.* Richard finds it all so revolting. No matter how much his heart thrums in his chest.

Beau should never have come back.

The drive home is very quiet, nothing but the patter of rain on the windshield. Numbness engulfs him, spreading like ice through his veins.

I have nothing left to give. That's not entirely true.

Richard knew that if it came down to it, he would give his soul.

~

THIS SHIT has to stop.

Richard fumes silently, glaring down at the invoice in his hands. It's done. Nothing they can do about it, and the dates are already booked.

What the fuck? Richard wants to scream.

"No, refund them—give the money back—"

"I'm sorry, Mr. Clayson. It's already done. You have six months of physical therapy booked and paid for. I can see if I can track down the person who paid, but as you know, we accept payments from third party individuals—"

Richard slams the phone down.

Fuck. He pinches the bridge of his nose, then scrubs his face violently. Drug money. What the hell is Beau thinking?

Is he using Richard again?

The thought is like a spear to his chest. It makes him want to crumple in agony after everything he's done. Everything he's given up just for Beau.

Whatever it is, he won't stand for it. Beau isn't fucking with him ever again.

He's got nothing.

Old brittle memories, falling like sand through his fingertips. A body that doesn't function, a family that hates him to his core.

Nothing but secrets and lies, whispering in the dark. Desperately chasing shadow and a thought. Not anymore. How terrible it is to willingly fall in love with a monster.

Nostrils flaring, he rips open the front door, storming out of his apartment building. The sky has cleared; it's hot and stuffy, the heat like a thick haze around him.

Richard drives with a deadly purpose.

Beau didn't leave any contact information, but he knows exactly where to find him.

In the lion's den.

He parks in front of the bar and yanks the front door open. The few men stare at him curiously, their gazes linger on his pronounced limp and awkward movements.

Richard couldn't give a fuck.

The bar is lively, heady with smoke and sweat. He makes his way through the crowd, hordes of men in leather jackets, rippling muscles, and harsh expressions. Richard grits his teeth, rage coursing through him.

Long ago, he would have postured, strutting around with his badge like a peacock, daring any of these fuckers to look at him twice. Now he slumps, body curled inward as several men pass him without a single glance.

As a civilian, he's nobody. Just a man with a cane and bad leg.

Richard wishes he could melt into the bar, dissipate like smoke in the air, weaving through the patrons. But, he can't.

Not with fury threatening to burn him alive.

Richard stalks forward, hand clenching at his side. He glances around, taking in the large spacious bar with several pool tables. Avery kept the place in good condition. Even after he was arrested for human trafficking, it seems the bar was sold to the highest bidder.

Hyena laughter spreads throughout the room. Neil sits leisurely in a booth, surrounded by his pack brothers.

Copper eyes wide and inquisitive, threatening deep pools of molten amber. Richard takes him in, noting the wide grin, sharp like the edge of a knife.

Sewer rats.

Richard marches toward them, eyes blazing with hatred. A man steps in front of him, blocking his view. His leather jacket stretches across his board frame, and light bounces off the skin of his head. "Can I help you?"

"I need to speak with Beau."

The man grins, wicked and salacious. "Don't we all."

He can't go through this again. The paranoia, the ache, feeling like his heart is being carved out of his chest. He just can't.

"I need to speak to him."

"Sorry, but he's indisposed at the moment..."

Those words leave nothing to the imagination.

Beau is still whoring. The thought rips through him, unraveling different parts until it punches him in the gut. No.

Not after everything. Not after prison and Mason, all those years he thought Creed might step up and behave like his older brother.

Turns out he was wrong. Richard's stomach flips. It loops so tightly he nearly retches. What kind of hell is this? Where he free's Beau only to throw him from one cage to another.

How sickening.

Yet, Beau rejected him. *I've never loved you*. The words wrap around his heart like barbwire. If he had stayed, Richard would have moved heaven and earth to ensure his safety.

To make sure he lived a normal life.

But, he didn't. Beau left with Creed and the cartels hot on their heels. That tells him enough. Beau would rather spend the rest of his life on his knees sucking dick than accept any of the help Richard has to offer.

It's maddening.

The demon comes then, swarming around him like a cloak of shadow, comforting and familiar. Richard welcomes the creature; he allows it to embrace him like a long-lost friend. And then the being curls its blackened claws around his neck.

"But… if you're willing to pay extra, I'm sure I can book you in—"

Richard punches him in the face.

Chapter 18

ALL HELL BREAKS LOOSE.

Several men whip out their firearms, guns cocked, and pointed straight at his head. Richard levels them, gaze fierce as thunder rips across the sky outside.

Let them all come, he thinks savagely. He yearns for it.

To see blood bursting out from veins and skin, to watch it flow sleek and copious, soaking the maroon rug. Neil stands slowly, cigar caught between his lips.

He descends like a puma toward its prey.

Richard is ready to spring at any movement.

"Let him through, Tanner," a voice says from the back.

The man Richard hit steps aside. His nose is bleeding profusely; his gun is pointed straight at his head.

Beau emerges from the darkness covered in a film of sweat, and a choker is clasped around his neck, making it look long and endless.

Neil approaches Beau, and he leans down to whisper into his ear, large hands sprawled across his lower back. "Problem?"

"Not at all."

They share a look before Neil smiles and backs away. "Keep it that way."

All of the men dissipate, withdrawing their guns and returning to their game of pool and drinking beer. However, their eyes remain watchful, sinister.

Richard just declared war.

"This way," Beau says, disappearing behind a thick black curtain. Richard fumbles his way inside, fuming visibly.

Beau leads him to a large office with a nice plush chair and mahogany desk. He takes a seat behind it like he owns the place.

Richard doesn't waste time. He throws bills and invoices on the table, hands trembling from the adrenaline rushing through him. "Take the money back. I don't want it."

Beau regards him, threading his hands together on the desk.

"I don't want the physical therapy—I don't want your fucking charity. Take it all fucking back. I don't need it," Richard barks.

"No."

Richard wants to break his neck.

"You fucking brat!"

Beau gets up swiftly, walking around the table to stand in front of him. "I won't take it back, not now or ever."

"I don't want it—"

"You *need* it," Beau says, his voice softening. "*Richard*—"

Suddenly he's underwater, swimming in currents that are trying to drag him under. For so long, he's wanted this moment. Beau with him, always and forever. Their love is the most precious thing he's ever been gifted in the whole world.

"Don't."

"I'm back." Beau looks deep into his eyes, pleading. "For good. I'm not leaving again."

"Bullshit."

Beau stiffens. "I can explain everything to you if you just listen."

"Stay the fuck away from me. I don't want to hear anything you have to say—"

"Wow," a voice says behind them. "Y'all bickering like an old married couple."

Richard freezes, then turns around, eyes narrowing.

Neil chuckles, sauntering into the room. "Got half the men out there wondering what's going on. I asked you before if we had a problem. It seems I was correct."

Beau's lips thin into a hard line. "No problem."

"None whatsoever," Richard deadpans.

"I know you." Neil studies his features, his grin widening. "You're that man from the diner. The one Maybelle was talking to... well shit, anyone who can take out that many Bandidos without breaking a sweat has my respect."

So, he does know Maybelle.

Christ, he wants no part of this. Whatever twisted game they had going on, Richard wants out. He's too tired to get wrapped up in all this shit again.

Beau gazes at him intensely. "I meant what I said, Richard. I'm here for good."

You shouldn't be, Richard wants to scream. This place is a black sucking hole, a vortex so thick and vast that there's no way ever to break through. Now Beau is back, whoring and selling drugs as if everything he sacrificed is worth nothing.

It's too revolting.

To release a bird only to see it shot down again. The shame of it all. The disgrace. Richard can't take it. On top of that, to have the money Beau makes through dubious means used *for* him as a kind of peace offering?

How can he ever accept it? Knowing the depravity Beau went through to get it. Better to cut it off at the root. No way in hell he'll ever accept money from Beau or anyone in this vicinity.

He'd rather be dead.

"So did I," Richard replies. "I don't want anything to do—"

"One day," Beau interrupts him. "That's all I'm asking for. Let me explain."

There's nothing to explain. Things are the same. Nothing will ever change. Richard bites back a scathing reply, hands curling at his side.

What does he gain from this? He'll only entangle himself further in Beau's web of lies. He's done so before, willing to throw himself off a cliff just to see Beau smile.

Richard relents before he's even conscious of it.

Beau looks so serene, face smooth and timeless, thick black hair curling around his nape and forehead. Even with the fury threatening to burn him alive, Richard finds him so beautiful.

"Fine."

Beau visibly relaxes, then takes the receipts and invoices off the table. He thumbs them, removing the crinkles from the paper. "Richard, I... things are different now. I swear it."

Richard desperately wants to believe him.

But deep down, he can't. Not with Neil leering beside him, smoking a cigar, eyes greedily taking in the free show. Are they fucking? Is he like Mason? Does he cut Beau to pieces at night and sell him to his men during the day?

Richard nods once, then walks out the door without another word.

One day. It seems like a lifetime.

CHAPTER 19

SHADE BECOMES A LUXURY in the summer heat.

Richard leans back in the lawn chair, taking in the vibrant hues of the backyard. It's been a while since he's been back here. Not since the divorce was finalized, anyway.

Lana has planted new trees, perennials sprout here and there, making the garden livelier. Ida tosses an air ball back and forth, while Roy mans the grill.

"How are you?" she asks, auburn hair tumbling down her back.

"I'm good." Enduring.

"That's good," Lana says, and then sighs. "I'm sorry about Kyle."

Richard shrugs, sipping his lemonade.

Kyle had taken one look at him and stormed upstairs, refusing to come out of his room for the rest of the night. Even Ida had stared at him, eyes wide and fearful.

These things happen.

Richard couldn't hide the hurt that flickered in his eyes. Yet, he remained impassive, playing with Ida when his knee allowed it and making small talk with Lana and Roy.

Things aren't the same.

There's too much space between them, a vast canyon stretching miles upon miles. Lana looks beautiful, softer than ever before. Longing for what they had pangs in his chest. Richard still wants to pummel Roy's face in for sleeping with his wife.

Then again, the feeling might be mutual.

"How are you?" Richard asks, grasping at straws. When did things become so awkward? Probably when Lana kept his kids away from him for months on end. Or when he cheated on her with an underage prostitute.

"Better," she says tightly. "Kyle is still getting bullied at school..." She fiddles with her ring finger, and Richard jolts when he notices the empty space.

He took his off months ago. But, for some strange reason seeing her without it saddens him.

"I don't know... I reckon I can try Gainesville for a teaching position... things are difficult. I haven't taught in almost ten years, and curriculums aren't the same. They're saying I may need more schooling."

Richard frowns. "Why go back to work? Roy can cover any expenses the kids need—"

"For independence," Lana cuts him off. "I don't want to be... *dependent* on anyone ever again."

Oh. That makes sense.

Richard is a jackass for not thinking about that. Lana deserved to have her career and not be fearful of where the money will come from. After he went to prison, she was severely impacted, and if it wasn't for Roy, she might have lost the house.

"Sorry," Richard says quietly. "That question was insensitive."

"It's fine... we've been going to church lately... Pastor Henry gives a good sermon. You should join us sometime."

"I'd like that."

They smile at each other.

"You're a good man, Richard," she responds. "I've never believed otherwise. Regardless of what you've done. I know you always have people's best interest at heart."

She knows him too well.

Richard's throat clogs with emotions. If he's so good, then why can't she accept him for who he is? Why must he always beg for scraps?

It's been months since he's seen his family. Kyle's grown so much. Richard is scared he'll miss the important times in his life when he will desperately need his father.

"Even though I'm gay," Richard replies. "Is that why you've kept me away?"

"That isn't at all what I meant."

"Then why—"

"I'm not comfortable with it," Lana replies candidly. "Especially now that *he's* back. It doesn't seem right to have him around the kids just yet—"

"I'm not seeing him," Richard grunts.

Lana's hand trembles. She cups her mouth, tears brimming in her eyes. "Richard," she says. "Beau was... *Christ*—he was a child... I don't blame him. Not for everything that happened. I used to, and it was wrong. He did what he needed to survive. What Mason did... it's sickening. I don't mind you are... *that way*... But to ask me to accept your relationship after you cheated and lied is something else. I need more time."

"Fair enough," Richard says. What more can he ask for? "Take all the time you need, but I'd like to be in my children's lives. That's all I'm asking for."

Lana remains quiet.

"I'd like that too," she says finally.

~

"LOOKS GOOD," Richard says, standing next to Roy at the grill.

"Thanks." Roy chuckles. "Someone has to cook around here. If I didn't, I'm sure Kyle and Ida would starve to death."

"I know," Richard says. "I once caught Lana putting the salad in the microwave."

"I'm honestly convinced she uses the smoke alarm as a cooking timer."

Richard laughs, shaking his head. "Good thing you're here then. Lord knows I've been the primary cook for years."

"Is it just me, or has it gotten worse?" Roy mutters. "At this point, Ida and Kyle automatically head for the dinner table every time they hear a fire truck siren."

Richard chuckles, then quickly glances around to make sure Lana isn't nearby. "Seriously, thank you for this. I appreciate it."

"No problem, brother," Roy says. "We can put work aside for a moment and just have a family BBQ. I'm sorry about Kyle, man, but he'll come around. It's just those kids at school."

"I know." Richard sips his lemonade. He's been so afraid to ask exactly what is being said, but he can guess just as well. "I need to explain things to him... I fear he still doesn't understand."

Roy snorts. "What's there to explain? You did your time. That's all that matters. Nothing more and nothing less."

"Yeah... but he may not understand... that I am gay... but that doesn't make me any different—"

"Oh, well, he doesn't need to know about *that* stuff," Roy says quickly. "Just leave him be for the time being."

Richard swallows, staring down at his drink.

Roy and Lana don't want him to tell Kyle. That explains the avoidance and why they've both kept him from coming around. It wasn't so much that he killed Mason, but all the things leading up to it.

He sighs deeply. There's no point in arguing. As much as he wants to rage against them for trying to stop him from coming out to his son, he knows it'll only cause more trouble.

He can wait to tell Kyle. By then, their relationship should be better.

CHAPTER 20

IT'S ALL WRONG, THOUGH.

Disappointment sweeps over him. Lana and Roy have their reasons. He just has to trust they are in Kyle's best interest. Richard clears his throat.

"How's the case going?"

Roy perks up. "There have been some interesting developments as of late."

"Such as?"

"Maybelle came down to the station to make her statement."

That's surprising. Good for her. Pride swells up within him. "I'm glad she did the right thing."

"Yeah." Roy sighs. "Poor girl... Look, I should have listened when you told me about it. Just... was too wrapped up in my own shit."

"It's alright." It's not.

"Still," Roy replies. "You've always been the better cop, hell, that's why you were the sheriff... anyway... I got her statement, and she said that Damian and Casey got into a big fight at the bar around eleven pm, and Maybelle told Damian she would drive him home... that's when things escalated."

"I see." Richard didn't need the details. He already got most of it from Maybelle.

"Bastard," Roy curses, then shakes his head. "I arrested him on sexual assault, but in terms of the murder, he couldn't have done it. Casey's death was between one and two am. That's when Maybelle said they were together."

"So why confess? Unless... he's protecting someone."

"My thoughts exactly... I did some more digging. Turns out Avery went bankrupt in prison, selling off all his properties, including the tailor shop and the bar. As of two months ago, the ownership is in the name of Neil Shaw."

"No shit," Richard says. What the fuck? Does he own the bar? Then that must mean he's whoring Beau out on the side.

He grits his teeth, stomach rolling with nausea. The sick bastard.

"You think it's connected to Casey?"

"Damn straight," Roy says. "A few months before Casey's death, her son joined the Rebel Brotherhood. On the night of the murder, Casey and Damian got into a fight at the bar, the one Avery used to own. That's the night Maybelle said Damian molested her. So, unless he has a doppelganger, there's no way he did that, then made it back to the precinct and killed his mother."

Then why did they both say they killed her? It just isn't adding up. Unless they are both trying to protect someone else. Maybelle working with the man that molested her doesn't make much sense either. Roy said they left around eleven pm and the murder took place a couple of hours afterward. It wouldn't be a stretch for Damian to molest Maybelle then return to the precinct to attack his mother.

Perhaps, Damian doesn't know Maybelle confessed?

"So, what do you need me for?"

"I'm hitting one dead end after the next. I know I'm not supposed to say stuff, but I could use your help."

"Oh really?" Richard scoffs. "I was a suspect not that long ago."

"You still are, but that doesn't mean you aren't a damn good detective. You were top of your class, Richard. Plus, you know I could never wrap my head around this stuff—"

"Yeah, yeah." Richard waves his hand dismissively. "What do you need?"

"An informant," Roy says. "Someone who can infiltrate the Rebel Brotherhood and gather all the information we need to bring them down. If it's a turf war against the Bandidos, then it must be over drugs. I need hard evidence to search the premises, though. Right now, nobody's talking. It was different with the Moonshiners. Back then, we had Callie and Patricia, but these men are like ghosts. I've run nearly half a dozen background checks, and nothing is showing up."

"I'm not going to be your fucking snitch," Richard snaps.

"Not a snitch." Roy rolls his eyes. "I ain't asking you to fucking snitch, just be my eyes and ears. CIs aren't that common in these parts—"

"Sounds like another term for snitch to me."

"This is serious. If we've got a fucking turf war, then the cartels are going to catch wind of it. That'll bring a hailstorm of shit nobody wants to deal with."

"I'm not doing it," Richard grits out. "It could go wrong so many ways. They already suspected me. Once it gets around that I'm an ex-cop, I'll be dead for sure. You're better off doing things clean. The Rebel Brotherhood can sniff that shit out a mile away."

"Clean? How?"

"Watch them," Richard says. "Keep tabs on Neil, heavy surveillance. That's the only way you're going to catch them in the act."

"Too much manpower," Roy replies. "I've got Isaac and Houston working the case on Casey. Then I've got Hiromi and Tanya on patrols. I ain't got much of a team left—"

"Rotate," Richard interrupts. "Put Houston and Tanya on patrols and Isaac and Hiromi on the case. Despite them not getting along, Hiromi and Isaac work well together."

"Man, they're like oil and water." Roy sighs. "But you're right. Okay, then I can personally oversee the surveillance of the club."

They lapse into silence.

It's difficult to wrap his head around everything. Neil owns the bar. That explains why the Rebel Brotherhood uses it as their base, but then again, how did Maybelle get mixed up in it all? It doesn't seem like a place she would frequent.

"Put it out of your mind for now," Roy says, then starts piling steak and burgers on a plate. "Let's just enjoy the rest of the day. Food's ready!"

Lana calls Ida and Kyle for dinner.

"You're doing the right thing, brother." Roy smiles. "We're going to be a family again, you'll see. It'll be like how it was before, in the good old days."

Before all that gay shit.

He doesn't say it, but Richard can taste the words nonetheless. The lemonade turns to cider vinegar and the sun into a blazing fire ball, melting the flesh of his bones.

"Sure."

CHAPTER 21

BEAU COMES.

Like he always does.

Richard is no stranger to these things.

A huge swathe of destruction, almost as if nothing had stood before it and lived to tell the tale. It's no surprise when he finds Beau at his doorstep, leaning against the wooden pillar with a face of utter nonchalance.

Smoke curling around his lips as he takes a long drag of his cigarette. Cool emerald eyes sparkling with mischief. His hair, black and straight, moves as soft prairie grass in summer wind, strands glowing in the twilight.

"One day."

Richard swallows, eyes flickering down to his thin lips wrapped around the cigarette. He drags his eyes away.

"Fine."

Beau steps in without an invitation. Audacious. Presumptuous. He smirks as if something good is about to happen. As if he's already won.

The world falls through Richard's feet.

"No." Richard's defensive, not ready to have Beau in his space again. "Let's take a walk."

Beau regards him, eyes wrinkling with mirth. "Okay. I have something to show you anyway."

He leaves, pivoting sharply and disappearing down the hall. Richard grabs his cane, stuffs whatever he needs in his pockets, and follows him out.

~

THEY TAKE separate vehicles.

Richard follows Beau in his beat-up Ford F-150 keeping a wide birth between them. After several sharp twists and turns, he knows exactly where Beau is going.

The auto shop looks different.

Richard climbs out of his truck, taking in the profound changes. Several men lounge around. They nod to Beau as he gets off his bike and enters through the main doors.

The shop is large, spacious, with brand new equipment. It's fully furnished with tasteful decoration and a large couch for customers. A lady at the desk smiles cheekily, eyes lighting up as Beau draws near.

Beau leans behind the counter, taking some receipts and paperwork with him.

"I'll be in the office."

"Sure thang," she drawls, popping her cherry gum.

Beau leads him to the back. Richard marvels at the vinyl floors, shining in the fluorescent lights. The mechanics look professional, not at all like the wayward back alley ones Gary used to employ.

They're competent, charlatans of their craft, and eager to assist. Beau walks confidently down a long corridor; it smells faintly of fresh paint and petroleum. They enter a large office. Once again, he takes his seat behind the desk.

Like he owns it.

Richard's jaw works, eyes narrowing suspiciously. "What is this?"

Beau tosses the documents on the table. "Have a look."

He reluctantly peers down at the pages, noticing the fancy cursive letter heading and the thick writing. *B. Blackwell's Auto shop*.

This is old news. Roy already told him that Beau had bought the auto shop. Yet, a wave of pride flows through him.

Richard smiles, thumbing the lettering in awe. *He did it*. Finally made something of himself. It's wonderful that Beau did all of this in a short amount of time.

The question is *how*? The smile fades, his mood damping more and more with confusion. If Beau bought the auto shop, why does he hang around Neil and his men? None of it makes any sense. If he owns the auto shop, where did he get the money from?

Oh.

"You can't give the money back," Richard says slowly. "Because you've already spent it."

Beau nods, leaning back in his chair.

"I don't understand." Roy told him that the bar was owned by Neil Shaw and that Avery went bankrupt in prison, selling off all his properties, including the tailor shop and the bar. How did Beau buy it? Are they business partners?

Richard taps his fingers on the table deep in thought.

Unless...Beau bought it off of Neil recently.

"He sold it to me two weeks ago," Beau explains. "My funds were tied up in investments and I asked him to buy it for me while it was on the market for cheap."

"Avery's bar too?"

"Yup."

"And the tailor shop?"

"Damn straight."

"Why?" Richard asks.

"Because fuck them. Fuck them all," Beau mutters darkly.

Those bastards took everything from him. Forced him into prostitution, raped him repeatedly. Why shouldn't he take their businesses? It's the least he can do. Richard understands, on some sick level, that Beau is slowly reclaiming everything he's lost from this town and turning it around.

"Well..." Richard says. "Congratulations. It looks great."

Beau doesn't reply.

"So... that explains a lot ..." Richard's at a loss of words. If Beau is using the auto shop to funnel in drug money, that explains how he could get it up and running in such a short amount of time. "Nobody questioned why you wanted to buy the property?"

"They were on the verge of bankruptcy," Beau responds easily.

"I see." That means the property sold for cheap, way under market value. Beau bought it, fixed it up, and now it's worth twice as much as he bought it for. "Smart."

Beau shrugs like it's not. Like owning three businesses is a cakewalk. It's easy confidence, one that Richard can't help but envy.

"So, Neil—"

"There's something I want you to see." Beau gets up quickly.

Richard frowns but follows him toward the garage. Several men look at him inquisitively, but they don't comment when Beau leads him toward the back. Glass shards litter the floor of one of the rooms; the window is smashed, and it looks like several pieces of equipment have been stolen.

Richard crouches, thumbing the debris and dirt from the window. "Did you report it?"

Beau nods, taking a look around. "One of the guys noticed a few days ago when he came back here to look for a wrench."

Whoever broke in must have stolen the murder weapon. That's the only way it makes sense. Still, the motive to kill Casey is unclear.

Richard stands up, his knee throbbing from bending down too long. "I see."

"You hungry?" Beau asks tentatively, "Let's go to dinner. My treat."

Richard knows he shouldn't.

Everything about Beau is the same, right down to his exasperating impenetrability. He's already spent too long in Beau's vicinity, trapped helplessly in his gravitational pull. The sky darkens, the stretch of twilight a tangible beacon of the stars to come.

Beau pins him with his gaze, lips pulled over sharp teeth.

Richard's a bird, caught between the jaws of a cat. One wrong move, and his neck snaps. Yet, there's nowhere else he'd rather be.

"Alright."

CHAPTER 22

THE DINER IS WARM, intimate.

Richard settles down in the plush seats, taking in the clay brick walls and huge stone beams.

It's a modern restaurant near the outskirts of Byrmonville. A new development, spreading through the ashes of decay. Gentrification came swift through the town, sweeping away the old weepy mills and vacant lands with bigger and better things.

It's a quiet evening. Most of the diner is empty except for the bar area. Richard orders some ice tea, along with a burger and fries. Beau surveys the menu, then orders a large pitcher of beer and some wings. It's nice.

A lot tamer than he excepted.

"The money..." Richard says low to avoid anyone overhearing them. "You know I can't accept it."

Beau fidgets, boney fingers tearing at the paper napkins. "Why not?"

Why not, indeed? He flounders, not expecting that response or the genuine hurt that flickers across his face.

"It's not legal money." Richard clears his throat. "You're laundering it through your business, which I suspect is something you learned from Enos."

"I made it legit."

Richard raises an eyebrow. "How?"

Their drinks arrive, and Beau takes a long sip. "Creed was a bastard. The fucker would have gotten us killed, so I did what I needed to do. After he died, I invested it in some stocks, traded it several times over, and cleaned it through other business ventures. After that, I bought the auto shop, the bar, and the tailor shop. It's legit."

Holy shit.

Richard swallows, tongue like lead in his mouth. Beau took half a million dollars of dirty money and cleaned it, filtered it through the system, and made it legitimate.

"They'll never trace it," Beau continues. "I made sure of it."

They fall silent.

Richard's too busy mulling things over.

It's still puzzling. Why would Beau come back? What does he gain from relieving those horrific memories? Wasn't it at Gary's auto shop that he was repeatedly raped? His back cut so viciously while Gary used it as lube while he masturbated? Or Avery's pub? Where Patricia, Callie, and Beau were passed between the men like rag dolls?

"Mason's old house—"

"Bulldozed," Beau chimes in, taking a long swing of his drink. "I couldn't stand the sight of that fucking place."

Revenge is a knife with rusty edges, a disfigurement of shame and disgrace so sharp it can slice through anything. Richard knows the feeling well.

Hatred is a cloak; one the demon resides in. Only to be released in the direst of circumstances. "You were very young... perhaps... some of the things they did you may forget."

"I remember *everything* they did to me," Beau rages, hands curling into fists. "I won't fucking rest until every wrong is righted. Those sick fucks deserved everything they got."

There are things you can teach. Others you cannot.

Richard knows this. Steps are easy, straightforward, relatively speaking. Street smartness and cleverness can be practiced and executed thoroughly. Even killing can be mastered.

Yet, *will* can never be taught.

Especially a will so fierce it fights past pain. Richard can see it all now. The rage hidden within the depths of his gaze, a hatred so deep it burrows under his skin.

The will of a dying tiger.

. No teenager should have it. No young adult should nurture it.

This one does.

Cradling the fire until it blazes beneath. That same fury coils deep inside Richard, familiar and steady, comforting like the demon's breath against his cheek.

Their salacious relationship ends—here and right fucking now. Mason's face flashes before his eyes. *This disgusting creature is a threat, contaminating his town and everything he holds dear.*

Good God—he could kill him again. Richard holds his breath behind pursed lips, and relief washes over him. He sighs, long and deep, letting out a shaky laugh.

Maybe this is where things were headed all along—to kill a demon, he has to become one.

It's all so overwhelming.

To learn that not only is his ex-fairy lover not whoring himself out, but he is also a successful business owner. How wrong he was.

How mad he was.

To think after all these years, everything stays the same. Richard smiles, his heart flayed, raw and beaten, but thumping rapidly.

Beau looks at him with wide-set eyes and a knowing gaze. All his questions answered, all fears put to rest. Richard is flying higher than a kite, soaring out of this world and into the next.

"You're free," he says with a manic grin. "You're free."

Beau laughs, shaking his head. "Yeah. I guess I am."

~

"THANK YOU."

It's late. Nearly after midnight. Richard is fuzzy with emotions, wistful, light as a feather dancing through the wind. He toys with his keys, reluctant to go.

"Anytime." Beau leans forward, bouncing on the balls of his feet, eyes glassy from all the beer he's consumed. They gaze at each other. Richard's hand grips the doorknob tightly.

He shouldn't want this.

To shove Beau against the wall and devour him, to slip his tongue into his sleek cavern and chase the taste of beer on his lips.

Of all the things he remembers, the first and most prominent is their time at the lagoon. The look of pure freedom, Beau's wide striking ivory teeth, his glistening body caught in the sunlight.

Beau's features exude radiance that transcends above all else. Richard's heart may very well burst with the magnitude of emotions.

"Beau." His heart sings.

Christ, he could ensnare his love. Trap him and strip him bare of those unsightly leather clothes. The blackened fabric hides too much. Richard yearns to trace his tongue over every inch of skin, to map the masculine planes of his smooth ceramic body.

How can Beau survive the force of his love?

The demon would wrap around him fully, encase his body into a box and compress it until each of his bones were crushed.

Beau would surely collapse beneath the tension, his brittle bones no match for the enormous supernatural begin.

The air sparks between them, crackling amidst the thundering in his ears. Beau tilts forward, and his whole body aligns with Richard's until the space between them becomes a hairbreadth.

"Ask me why I came back," Beau whispers, warm breath cascading over his cheek. He reaches between them, pressing his palm against the front part of Richard's jeans.

His traitorous cock swells.

The heat of his palm bleeds through the fabric. It's hot and heady, making him flush with excitement. Beau noses his cheek, thin lips curling upwards.

"Why?" Richard asks, his voice thick like gravel.

"You. Always for you."

CHAPTER 23

THEIR LIPS SMASH TOGETHER.

Richard groans, trying to flatten and destroy his mouth all at once. Beau hungrily pushes back, mouth open and tongue plunging past his clenched teeth, into the moist space between. Richard grabs a handful of baby hairs at the base of Beau's skull to ground him into reality.

Richard drives his tongue deeper.

Their tongues battle back and forth savagely, trying to pin each other. It's an explosion, the best flavors in all the universe bundled into one.

Beau tastes so sweet, rose petal lips, supple and decadent.

Soft sounds escape Beau's mouth. He pants jaggedly through his nose as his hands roam all over Richard's chest. Richard yearns to kiss away those stains. Beau grunts, yanking him closer with his hands on his waist, and licks his tongue over the roof of his mouth, pulling back to suck on his bottom lip and to bite down.

Richard lets out a noise, somewhere between surprised and aroused.

Nipping at his skin, Beau lavishes the column of his neck with wet and urgent kisses. He moves behind his earlobe, sucking hard enough to make Richard's toes curl.

Fuck. He melts.

Right between the floorboards, between space and time, and Beau's meaty thighs. It's so wonderfully delicious. Richard moans loud, fisting Beau's hair and dragging him back for another searing kiss.

Beau reaches downward, kneading Richard's cock through the fabric of his jeans. He rolls it between his greedy fingers, causing Richard to see stars. Things are turning quicker than he originally thought, and Richard knows that he can't let things go any further.

A private sort of shame begins to reside in him.

It sets up home in the pit of his chest, shoving aside heartstrings to extend its tendrils. Wrapped around his heart, his shame controls him.

Promise me you won't see him. Promise me.

Richard tears his mouth away.

They're both breathless, chests rising and falling rapidly as they draw air into their hungry lungs. He's delirious, faint with excitement and passion coursing through his veins.

It's stupendous.

Yet, at the same time, he doesn't want to lie anymore. He promised his family he wouldn't see Beau ever again. If he does, he knows he will be lost forever.

He can't go through that again.

Beau rushes back in, kissing him soundly on the lips, taking advantage of their momentary reprieve to seal their lips together.

Richard inhales sharply, nostrils flaring at the boldness of the kiss. He places a firm hand on Beau's chest and shoves. "Beau, stop—"

"Why?" Beau leans in, dragging his tongue across the coarse hairs on his unshaven cheek. "Please, it's been so long—"

"Don't." He'll die if he does. "We can't."

Beau gazes at him, eyes searching.

A multitude of emotions race across his face: anger, betrayal, bitterness, and resentment. Richard doesn't understand any of it.

"I came back *for* you," Beau says slowly. "I'm here for good."

Richard's breath catches.

No. It's not true.

Did Beau come back to hell for him? Impossible. He moves further way, thoughts whirling with the realization that it probably is true.

"Look, if you feel guilty or you pity me—"

"I do," Beau cuts him off. "Of course, I feel fucking guilty. I never wanted—things changed and got so fucked. You never let me explain why—"

"I don't need to know." *I've never loved you*. "The reasons don't matter."

Beau looks as if he's been slapped. His eyes narrow as he straightens his jacket.

"I see."

Richard is ready to retreat.

He's fatigued, his knee slightly throbbing from standing for too long. It's time to rest. He needs to think. A lot is going on, and too many unknown variables need to be taken into consideration.

Richard needs to keep his distance; steer clear of this siren before it consumes him again. However, he knows he's powerless. If Beau seeks him out, he cannot help but respond.

"I'll contact you if anything else happens," Beau says, but his eyes dip down to his lips, suggesting otherwise.

"Yeah, okay."

Beau departs as swiftly as he came, like a typhoon on the horizon.

Leaving a sea of destruction in his wake.

~

"HOW'S THE pain?"

"Manageable," Richard says as the doctor examines the kneecap, stretching out his leg.

"You're lucky you can still walk," Dr. Trevor says, patting him on the back. The wrinkles around his eyes are deeper, more profound than ever before.

He's the oldest doctor in Byrmonville.

"Okay." Trevor smiles. "You can put your clothes on."

Richard stands up from the examination table and puts his jeans back on. He breathes slowly, focusing on putting one leg on and then the other, ignoring the sparks of pain shooting up his thigh.

"Do you want the goods news or the bad news?"

"Bad news." Richard sits down gingerly, rubbing his knee gently.

"Alright, son." Trevor sighs. "Bad news is that the torn cartilage is caught between the structures in your knee, which is causing the pain. We can keep up with the pain killers, but I'm afraid it's like pouring gasoline on a fire."

"Great. And the good news?"

"I heard the cartilage regeneration surgery was all paid for, so we can book you in as soon as possible—"

"I'm not accepting that payment," Richard responds through gritted teeth. "It was a mistake."

Trevor frowns, picking up his paperwork. "No, Kelly Ann says it's legitimate, everything paid in full, son."

"I know. I'll fix it. We can stick with the pain killers for now."

Trevor sighs deeply. "It's not advisable... Richard, at this point, with the way this is progressing... if you don't get that surgery, one day you may never walk again."

Richard's stomach drops. The words buzz around him before settling deep within his skin.

"Let me... I need to discuss it with my family... How long do I have?"

"I would say six months at most," Trevor says, then offers a weak smile. "Just call my office. Kelly Ann will set everything up."

"I will, thank you." He stands ready to leave.

"Richard," Trevor says. "We haven't discussed—"

"Not today." Richard grits his teeth, hands curling over his cane. He can't talk about it right now. It's far too distressing, with everything else piling on top.

Trevor gazes at him pitifully, hands toying with his pen. "It's malignant, son."

"I know."

Richard walks out the door. The world fades in and out as he ambles to his truck. It's a lovely day, sun high in the sky, warm breeze on his cheek.

The demon gazes at him through the review mirror.

Large red eyes with narrow slits. It looks worn, tired, as if all the fight is drained out completely. Richard knows the feeling.

His hand tremors slightly, white noise rings in his ears.

What can he truly offer Beau anyway?

Nothing but pain and heartache.

CHAPTER 24

THE HEATWAVE INVITES LONG and lazy summer days.

Richard lingers in the space between now and then. Hopelessly replaying that kiss over and over again.

He thumbs the place Beau touched, wistfully. It's too good to be true. He scratches his neck, and the coarse hairs bristle against his fingertips.

"Are you listening?"

No. Richard sighs, tapping his knuckles against his thigh. Roy insisted they meet again, this time at the local park.

He watches Ida play in the sandpit. She tosses the ball in the air; it bounces once before rolling away. Richard smiles softly at her frustrated pout.

"It's all speculative," Richard responds.

"Yeah, but shit, we need someone in there—"

"Not this again," Richard mutters, shaking his head. "If you dragged me out here to talk about being an informant, I'm going home."

Roy turns silent, biting his lower lip.

Ida runs over to them. "Baba! I want to go on the swings!"

"Alright, honey," Roy answers immediately, causing Richard to bristle. "I'll take you." He stands her up, then walks over to the swing set and helps her climb on. He pushes her several times, making exaggerated grunting noises each time.

Ida erupts with laughter.

Her auburn hair sways in the wind. Jealousy sparks inside Richard. Hot and furious. Baba. He is her father, not Roy. It burns him to his core.

Yet, Richard grins and bears it all.

After all, he deserves it. They return shortly. Ida sits down in the grass and plays quietly with her barbie dolls. Richard desperately wants to hold her, to bounce her on his knee and cradle her delicate body.

However, pain flares within his bones, making the ache nearly unbearable. Today isn't a good day.

"That's not why I called you here," Roy says quietly.

Richard turns to him, frowning deeply. "What is it? You have news about the case?"

"Not exactly," Roy says, looking away. "Look, I don't know how much of this public knowledge... I went over the case Casey was building, and I found out some information that I thought you should be privy to..."

"What information?"

"Turns out Enos ordered the hit on you in prison," Roy explains. "I don't know the details, but my guess is he got some of his crew together to assault you."

His vision blurs, racing back to that moment in time when everything fell to pieces. The rancid stretch of sweat as all the convicts huddled together, waiting for entry to their cells.

The blows came swift and unyielding. Richard can still feel the swing of metal smashing against his skin. His kneecap crushed, the sickening sound of bone cracking.

Blood. His and the demon's are covering the tile floors. And laughter, ruthless and malevolent as they continue their assault, long after his body has stilled completely.

How can he forget? The coma left him bedridden for years, learning basic functions and body movements. Beau. All of it for Beau.

Tears sting his eyes.

Richard shouldn't allow him to come back. Not now. Not after everything. Roy is right. They just got him back. Richard is a shell of his former self.

He swallows down his emotions, hands slightly tremoring. The kiss replays in his mind over and over again. What does Beau want?

"I see... now Enos is dead."

"Yeah," Roy says lowly. "Strange turn of events, don't you think?"

This shit again. "I didn't kill him."

"I'm not saying you did, brother." But he is. "I'm just saying it's odd, is all. They finally released his autopsy, and he died in the same way Casey did, blunt trauma to the head and cuts all over his body, fucker must have been alive while he was being slashed to pieces. Whoever did this is a sadistic fuck."

"Not as sadistic as Enos," Richard sneers.

"I agree with you on that, but—he was killed in prison. I don't know who would have that kind of authority, but none of the guards saw shit."

That means whoever killed Casey and Enos has serious connections. Fuck. Richard scrubs his face, learning over in his seat. "No leads?"

"Nothing besides Damian... someone posted bail, so he's out now. We're keeping a close eye on him."

No word about Beau and the cartels.

"And the wrench? Did you find out where that came from?"

"Not yet."

Richard debates telling Roy about his meeting with Beau. It would probably help the case, but it might also implicate Beau. "Look, perhaps you should look into anything reported stolen around the city."

Roy's eyes narrow. "Why would I do that?"

"Just try it and see what comes up." Richard evades the question. "I think something there might have some connection to the weapon that was used to hit Casey in the head."

"You seem confident about this. What aren't you telling me?"

He can't tell him. Not yet. Not until he's sure exactly where he stands on everything and how much Beau is involved with the Rebel Brotherhood.

"Just chasing a hunch is all," he replies flippantly. "I think the Rebel Brotherhood is involved. See what you can find on them. That'll be your best start."

Roy nods. "Okay, good. I like it... Are you sure you don't want to be an informant?"

Richard laughs, shaking his head. "I'm sure."

Roy smiles sadly at him. "I miss this, brother."

Clouds gather, blocking out the sun. Richard gazes at the skyline, feeling a deep pang in his chest. Things aren't the same.

Roy decimated his life.

Tore him out of the closet kicking and screaming, destroying his marriage and career in one fell swoop. Richard can still recall the manic glint in his eyes as if ruining his best friend's life gave him sick sadistic pleasure.

The bastard even got a promotion afterward.

Richard was the root of all evil, obstructing justice, sleeping with an underage prostitute, tampering with evidence. A cluster fuck of charges was thrown at him. All completely true.

He killed Mason. Fucked Beau and never looked back. Richard was a fraud. A sham sheriff, a wolf in sheep's clothing, a demon in human skin.

Yet, he missed the thrill.

Being on top. The level of respect given from strangers and friends alike. Being a cop was the blood in his veins, over fifteen years of service to his country. Starting a year after he was discharged from the military at eighteen.

"Me too. I miss it too."

CHAPTER 25

BRITTLE BONES, MEMORIES WORSENING by the day. Pain so swift it tears up his thigh, rendering him immobile for hours.

It's heaven. It's hell.

There's a quiet knock on his door. Richard glares at it, frown deepening. Today isn't a good today. Not with his head threatening to explode and his knee bursting in agony. The medication is slow, languid, almost like the summer heat.

It refuses to spread, to relieve the throbbing in his body. Richard takes his time; he grabs his cane, leaning heavily on it as he pops open the door.

Beau is back.

Snubbed nose, freckled chest, hands slowly caressing his naked neck. Richard's eyes feast upon him. Taking in the slow dip of his tongue as it drags across his lower lip.

He leans against the door again with a lecherous grin. "I'm not going anywhere."

Richard stiffens.

That's a dangerous thing to say. Especially to a demon. He takes those words, absorbs them, letting them sink into his skin. *Why now? Why not before?* Richard wants to scream.

Richard sighs long and deep, face heating with the weight of Beau's stare. His last words replaying in his ears. *I'll contact you if anything happens.*

"Something happened."

"You could say that."

He's caught off guard, stunned almost. Already? The exclaim is at the tip of his tongue. Beau shrugs, cool and languid like it's no big deal the cartels want him dead. "Have you eaten?"

This dance seems vaguely familiar. Not long ago, he was asking a dirty teenager wandering the side of the road the same question.

"I could eat."

"Then let's go for a drive."

Yeah, let's.

~

A THOUSAND-MILE stretch of silk-smooth road. Richard takes in the reflective greens of the landscape glowing brighter in the strengthening lights.

He lazily tips his head back, letting the breeze flow through his hair. It's quiet between them, but the silence is clean, welcomed. Richard keeps his eyes on the road and not on Beau's strong hands against the steering wheel.

The takeout smells delicious. The scent of fried chicken and grits wafts from the back seat. Richard isn't sure where they are going, but at this point, he doesn't care.

All that matters is the here and now.

He'll marvel at his absurdity later. Mistakes he's made unapologetically. The first is: allowing his ex-lover to drive his truck for everyone to see.

Beau parks in a lot near the edge of farmland, where wheat grass sways in the wind.

He grabs the food from the pack, passes Richard his meal, and then starts digging into his own.

Plastic forks scrape across paper plates. Richard licks the grease off his fingers, chuckling when ketchup stains his pants.

"Good?"

"Amazing," Richard responds, wiping his fingers with a napkin. "Thank you."

"Anytime."

Richard nods but doesn't comment on the weight of his words. It's unusual, this turn of events. He has never been the type to wear his heart on his sleeve, but with Beau, everything comes naturally. Now, however, he finds things are backward.

Beau looks at him and expects more. As if Richard is on hold, withholding himself and not at all being transparent. Which is true to some degree.

"They attacked one of our guys," Beau says. "I told Neil not to retaliate, but this is just the beginning."

"Does Roy know?" Richard asks.

"Yeah, he took all of our statements."

"Then you'll have to let the cops handle it—"

Beau turns to him. "They won't do anything about it."

"How do you know?"

Beau scoffs. "I just know. Trust me."

What do you want me to do about it? Richard wants to demand.

"I'm not a cop anymore. I can't help you."

"You're the only one that can," Beau replies seriously. "I know we can figure something out to get the cartels off the Rebel Brotherhood's back—"

There it is.

Some sick, demented game, where Richard will no doubt be set up for the fall. Richard's nostrils flare, anger boils inside him threatening to erupt.

"*We?*" Richard's hands curl into fists. "I'm not a part of this shit. I never was."

"Everyone is a part of it," Beau spits. "Not just you, but everyone you hold dear."

"What the fuck is that supposed to mean?" Richard snaps. "I'm sick of these games, Beau. You can't just come back, stir shit up, and walk away like you usually do."

"Is that what you think?" Beau demands. "That I would contact you just to fuck you over? I would have given anything to stay. Anything."

"But you didn't," Richard fumes. "So, what do you want now?"

"You."

Richard inhales sharply.

What the fuck? Beau turns to look at him, mouth drawn in stubborn determination. What is this? Richard's head whirls, vision blurring in and out. Some kind of joke? For all the years he's yearned for Beau to say the words, to acknowledge his affection only to have it thrown back in his face so cruelly.

Richard's hands clench, stomach roiling in despair.

Beau doesn't want him.

How could he? Especially when they barely know each other now. How could he want a monster? Richard took advantage of him, stuffed him with malice and hatred, then captured him and forced him to live in a cage.

Richard is a dying tiger, too worn and frail to fight against the raging storm around him.

"Take me home."

This conversation is over. Beau places the keys back in the ignition and pulls out of the parking spot at the edge of the lot.

CHAPTER 26

No questions are answered.

Nothing is resolved. Richard is beyond exasperated. He knows less now than he ever did before. The detective inside him is itching to get answers. It makes his skin crawl with anxiety.

Like tonguing an open sore inside his mouth.

He probes and licks at the wound, only to reel back in agony. Beau walks him to the front door, hands in his jeans, which hang low on his hips.

Richard takes in the dip of his collarbone, the wide set of his shoulders. His hair tussles, sweat pools on his upper lip and brow.

They have nothing more to say.

And yet, he lingers again.

Richard's heart lurches. The words that were spoken earlier make hope blossom where it should rot. *Does Beau care? Did he ever?* The words are ringing in his ears, white noise.

He would do it all again. He doesn't care. If it meant Beau could be finally free. He would spend eternity in prison. *They used to cut me.* Richard remembers the scars, ugly things, slicing up his entire back and forearms.

Mason used to use it for lubrication. The sick bastard.

Richard's chest tightens.

Their love is the fire raging in his veins, the impending cyclone in the skyline. It's inevitable, all-consuming.

He wants him badly. So very badly.

Richard's stomach clenches, dick hardening to the point of pain.

His impatience is growing, mounting every day. A spark of heat, a flash of skin drives him into a frenzy. Soon, very soon, they will be alone together.

Richard is nervous, his hands grow damp, and his throat dries at the thought. He wants soft kisses in the dark, lude moans, deep laughter.

Worst of all, he wants to consume Beau as if he will die of thirst if he doesn't.

These thoughts come like a tidal wave. And he knows like he's always known, that he would never grow tired of looking at him.

The slop of his nose, wide-set lips, and cheeks cut and chiseled. Although he is still very young, there is a semblance of hardness to his exterior, something akin to future manhood.

"I'm fucking shit up, aren't I?"

Completely. Beau sighs, staring at the ground dejected.

"Yes and no... look, if you want to continue... whatever this is... I need full transparency. Or else I can't help you. I can't protect you."

"Okay, I'll tell you... whatever you want to know."

"Good." Richard opens the front door to his apartment and gestures for Beau to come inside. "That's all I ask."

Beau steps over the threshold, his strides long and confident.

Richard's glad he decided to clean the day before. It still doesn't remove the faint smell of mildew from the windows or the yellowish paint on the walls. It's a far cry from their usual spot at the motel, but it's enough.

"Do you want something to drink?" It's hot. He's ready to tear off his shirt if only to get some reprieve from the heat. "I don't have an air conditioner."

Richard walks toward the sink and pours them both a glass of water. He drains his in one gulp and takes a stuttering breath.

"Water is fine," Beau whispers, his breath brushing against the nape of his neck. Richard starts, turning around sharply to find Beau pressed up against him.

Again.

"What are you doing?" Richard asks weakly.

Beau leans into him, touching his skin, tracing the sharpness of his cheekbones. His emerald eyes are gems up close, so wide and beautiful that Richard's breath catches.

"I am here, Richard. *Finally*."

Please, Beau begs with his body and words. Richard cracks, his mind splintering as it bleeds past into the present.

It's too late. He can't now. Richard runs his free hand up Beau's inner thigh, stopping when he reaches his sharp hip bones, rubbing his thumb in soothing circles.

"I can't be gentle."

He won't. Not now. Not after everything.

"I don't want you to be."

Richard's hands slither to the nape of his neck, fisting the hairs there and yanking his head back. "I can't share you. Not with Neil or anyone else in that Godforsaken club."

Beau gasps, mouth parting. "*Yes*."

"Promise me."

"I promise."

Richard brushes his thumb over Beau's cheeks, heart beating when he sees tears slip from his eyes. Fuck. Beau's tears are the most beautiful things he's ever seen.

His mind fractures, the frail pieces of his sanity disintegrating, he allows all the walls built around his heart to disintegrate.

Richard attacks Beau's mouth, kissing him until his mouth bleeds.

It's ruthless, quick, and strident, sumptuously melting his heart.

Like striking a match, everything ignites. They are kissing feverishly, passionately, trying to consume each other. Their lips and tongues clash fast and furious; he's so hard he could die.

They pant; Beau looks debouched with his face red and lips redder.

CHAPTER 27

THEY KISS AND KISS, Beau's hungry mouth finding him again and again.

Beau drops to his knees.

And Richard nearly faints. Thoughts swirl inside his head as the room spins. He recalls a night just like this four years ago, both of them covered by the night, and Beau's sleek lips wrapped out his aching cock.

Christ—Beau looks up at him under his thick lashes.

Richard cradles his face. He parts those lips with his thumb, forcing it through the wet cavern. Beau unbuttons his pants, impatiently pulling down his trousers, fingers trailing over his thighs and hips, over every bit of skin he can reach.

The demon sings then, causing the hairs on his arms to rise.

"Hands behind your back," Richard says, his voice gathering strength. Beau instantly obeys. "Open your mouth."

Beau's eyes never once leave his.

His lashes flutter when Richard threads fingers through his hair, holding his head in place as he feeds Beau his cock. He can feel Beau trembling from the effort of holding himself back, holding himself still and silent as Richard slowly fucks his mouth.

He's an expert, after all. Richard shudders at the thought.

Beau only makes an involuntary sound when Richard's cock hits the back of his throat.

"You can take it," Richard says, voice breaking.

He pulls Beau forward until he makes that noise again, then he tightens his grip on Beau's hair and listens to him breathe harshly through his nose.

Richard holds him there, not giving him any other way out, until Beau's throat finally relaxes enough for him to push right into that slick heat.

"Swallow," Richard commands, and Beau does.

His eyes squeeze shut as his throat works. It's almost too much. It's what they both need. Richard takes a steadying breath and shoves his cock even deeper, fucking Beau's throat until those little choking sounds take on a far more urgent edge.

Still, he keeps his hands firmly behind his back, obedient to the last. Then he looks up again, eyes bulging, black lashes sweeping across his pale cheek.

He grips Beau's chin, forcing his mouth open and filling it again.

Richard carefully wipes away his tears while Beau sucks his cock, his lips forming a tight seal as he bobs his head. He's unbearably lovely like this: on his knees, his mouth full, looking up at Richard with tears in his eyes. Needy, utterly trusting.

Pleasure curls through Richard—pleasure and something even sweeter, like distant thunder, or perhaps it's just the roar of his heartbeat. The night is cloudless and silent, broken only by his ragged breathing and the obscene slide of Beau's lips.

"You can use your hands," Richard says, thrusting his hips. "Go ahead."

Beau whimpers.

And instead of touching himself, his hands come around to grip Richard's legs. Fingers dig into the back of his thighs, moving up to grab his ass.

Beau uses this newfound leverage to pull him closer, throat working to take his cock even deeper. And absurdly enough, that's what finally sends Richard over the edge—the feeling of Beau clinging to him, both arms around his knees, sobbing silently as Richard fucks his throat raw and comes in his mouth.

Desire steals over Richard without warning, without fanfare, distant, and then suddenly he spills deep inside Beau's mouth.

His knees nearly buckle, hands shaking, with sweat covering his neck and face. God—the world spins as he struggles to remain upright.

Beau steadies him with a firm hand on his thigh, releasing his soft cock with an audible pop. It's obscene. So deliciously depraved. Richard yanks Beau upright, spinning them around until Beau crashes into the wall.

Richard kisses him deeply, tasting the salty sweetness of tears and spend on his lips and cheeks. He bites down into his collarbone, relishing the mewling sounds Beau makes.

He reaches between Beau's legs, pawing at the unmistakable damp patch on his pants. Richard pulls back, gripping Beau's narrow chin between his fingers, eyes questioning, searching.

Is this what you truly want? Richard wants to ask, but the words are stuck in his throat. He won't accept half of Beau. He can't. Before things were all wrong, Beau was far too young. Now things are different.

Perhaps, they can finally be together.

Beau stares back at him, eyes heavily hooded, blinking and winking in the dying day. *I am yours*, they say, as his hands reach to clutch his t-shit.

I am yours.

~

HAPPINESS.

What does Richard know about that? Happiness is not something to be bought or sold. Happiness isn't a painting. It's not something to be captured by ink on paper.

But perhaps it's something fleeting and melodious. The clear trill of a flute under the moonlight, sweet as rainwater on new spring leaves, or perhaps it's this right here, Beau in his arms, head nestled against his chest.

Paradise.

Richard watches him sleep, noting the shadows beneath his eyes. How long has it been since he found rest? Too long, it seems.

The sky is dark as night crawls near. Richard runs his hand across Beau's hand, marveling at the strands.

What happens next? He's got no clue.

But things can't be like they were before. He won't allow it. Tomorrow he'll tell Roy the truth, then move on to Lana.

His life begins and ends with Beau.

He won't have it any other way.

CHAPTER 28

RICHARD SPIRALS HEAVENWARD.

Morning comes gracefully, and sun rays flutter through his white curtains. A sense of serenity washes over him, a peace that nestles itself deep within his soul.

Beau stirs, emerald eyes looking luminous in the daylight. For an instant, he stares up at Richard, his fine-boned hands tracing his unshaven cheek.

It's a moment, but it feels like an eternity.

Richard kisses him, long and deep, relishing the taste of his fairy lover. Beau moans but pulls away. "Richard."

"I'm here."

"I have to go."

Oh. He nods stiffly. Beau runs several businesses. Of course, he is needed. Yet, he wants to beg him to stay a little longer.

"I can come back tonight."

"Okay." But he doesn't let him go, not just yet. "Where are you staying?"

"Depends," Beau answers vaguely. "Sometimes at the bar, other times I crash at the auto shop."

"I see."

A moment of silence, then he slowly removes his arms. "You can freshen up in the bathroom."

Beau nods then hops off the bed, stretching his arms over his head, and walks sleepily to the bathroom. Richard takes his medication, swallowing down each pill dutifully, along with a glass of water.

Once he's finished, he goes to the kitchen.

There's nothing to do. Beau doesn't have time for breakfast, and Richard's got nowhere to be. It's sad. He's almost tempted to follow Beau into work.

Beau steps out of the bedroom, shrugging on his leather jacket. "I'll come back around six. Maybe we can grab dinner again?"

"Sure." Richard watches him, heart pounding.

Beau kisses him softly. "I'll see you soon."

"Okay." Soon.

Beau leaves, taking his heart with him. Something settles in his chest, thick and hard, almost like a lump of burning hot coal.

It isn't until later he realizes that it's not affection but suspicion.

~

RICHARD TAKES a stroll.

His mind is in disarray. If he's going to tell Lana, rip apart his family again, he needs to make sure that it's *for* something. Unfortunately, Beau isn't giving him much to go on.

The cartels are closing in. Neil is a nefarious individual with a questionable past, and it seems as though they're deeply intertwined. He can't get one without the other.

The case isn't something he can easily solve overnight. He considers calling Roy but decides against it. He'll ask more questions, and Richard doesn't have any answers.

"Screw off!" someone screams.

Richard whips around, eyes widening when he sees Maybelle trying to wrench her arm away from her captive. He's moving before he can even think, fury blazing inside of him. "Let her go!"

Her captor reels back, then releases her arm.

"You're not supposed to come near me!" she cries. "You aren't supposed to come near me!"

"I'm sorry! I'm sorry!" the man says hysterically. "I just need to explain—I loved my mother. I would never hurt her! Please believe me! I never meant to hurt you either—I was drunk and stupid—"

Richard immediately steps in front of Maybelle, his entire body shaking in anger. "Back the fuck away."

"Please," he mutters pitifully. "I would *never* hurt her."

What the fuck?

Holy fuck. It's Damian. Casey's son.

Looking at him, he can tell how he's able to molest all those women. He's handsome, in a beach boy surfer kind of way, easily underestimated.

A wriggling worm. Richard despises him, and men like him. It is truly disgusting, to take and violate, to destroy lives all for the sake of their gain.

If he had his gun, he'd shoot the bastard and call it an accident. Rid the world of his toxicity. Without Casey to cover it up, he'll rot in prison for sure.

"The cops are on their way."

Richard reaches into his pocket and starts dialing. Damian remains on the ground, tears soaking his shirt.

"Why would you say I killed her? Why would you make me confess?" he spews over and over again.

"Shut up!" Maybelle yells at him, her face soaked with tears. "She was a monster! And so are you!"

What the hell is going on? Richard holds her back, steering her further onto the sidewalk and away from Damian. Did they plan this?

He recalls that night, Maybelle coming to him, rained drenched and sully. Confessing to murdering Casey in cold blood.

Richard effortlessly dismissed it for reasons that he realizes now are completely misogynistic. Maybelle and Casey were similar in weight and height. There's no way she'd be able to drag her from outside into the precinct.

But what if she had help?

Everything comes to a grinding halt. Beau's auto shop was broken into the day before. Some things went missing. What if it was the wrench? The weapon used to club Casey over the head?

What if Maybelle used the weapon and Damian dragged her body? That seems more plausible. Yet, that doesn't explain the strange cuts all over her body or the painting all over the wall.

They both had a motive, though.

Maybelle was furious about Casey threatening her and smothering evidence regarding her sexual assault. Perhaps, Casey got fed up, went to the bar to confront her son, and told him she wasn't going to assist in hiding it?

It still doesn't sound right.

Maybelle isn't a killer, neither is Damian. They aren't sadists. They hurt her. That much is clear, but maybe they hadn't meant to kill her? And dropped her off at the station in the hopes of someone finding her.

That means they were being watched. Whoever was watching them killed Casey.

Maybelle's face is ashen. She's trembling so hard her lips are nearly chattering.

"It's okay," Richard says soothingly. He doesn't try to touch her, knowing that right now, it won't be welcomed. "Roy is on his way. They'll arrest him."

"It's not right." She shakes her head manically. "He can't come near me—not after what we did—what he did—"

"Maybelle," Richard says sternly. "I need you to take deep breaths, in and out."

She gulps loudly, wringing her hands. "I didn't mean to, Richard. I didn't."

"I know," Richard says softly. "Try to calm down. We can talk when you feel better."

"He told us it was for the greater good," she continues. "That everything would be resolved with my daddy—he promised us—"

A siren's wail causes them both to stop.

Roy and Hiromi pull up in a police cruiser, both with their hands on their guns. Maybelle sprints forward, throwing her arms around Hiromi's neck tightly. Roy arrests Damian, putting him in the back of the car.

Two more cruisers pull up. He recognizes Isaac and Houston immediately. Roy approaches him slowly, taking off his aviator sunglasses. "What happened?"

Richard leads Roy away, gripping his cane tightly. "You need to make a move. Now."

"Talk to me, brother." Roy inclines his head.

"Maybelle and Damian didn't kill Casey, but I think they assaulted her."

"You mean—"

"Instead of looking for one suspect, you should be looking for three."

CHAPTER 29

"THIS IS INSANE," MONROE mutters, pacing back and forth in the tiny office. "My daughter had nothing to do with this."

"I beg to differ," Roy drawls. "Look, I don't want to arrest her, but things are just not adding up. She needs to talk, or else I can't protect her."

"Protect her?" Monroe sneers. "She's a child for Christ's sakes! My flesh and blood. Maybelle's always been decent toward you people. I've raised her right. That man defiled her. I should kill him where he stands."

Richard really shouldn't be here.

Yet, Roy insisted, claiming that he's a viable witness or some shit. It's pure crap.

"I'm not disputing that, hell, I've known Maybelle for as long as I can remember. Bonnie still tutors Kyle and babysits Ida, but the law is the law. I have to do my job."

"Blessed is the man who walks not in the counsel of the wicked, nor stands in the way of sinners, nor sits in the seat of scornful," Monroe replies strongly. "My daughter would never be caught up in such deceit. Check your facts, then check them again."

Richard's hand curls into a fist.

Monroe used to be someone he admired, almost like a father figure while growing up and struggling with his sexuality. Hell, the bastard even helped him get sober after his father disowned him. Richard will never forget the kindness he showed that day and every day afterward.

Until he found out Richard was queer.

Since then, he hasn't heard from Monroe. It's a miracle Bonnie and Maybelle still talk to him after Monroe banned him from the diner. His bigotry was well known. It's part of the reason why it took him so long to come out. He didn't want to lose the only father he had left.

In the end, he did anyway. He lost everything.

"Monroe," Roy pleads. "Be reasonable. If she doesn't talk, I'll have to arrest her. I don't want to do that. If she is withholding information regarding the case, it ain't right, and you know it."

"Since when did you take advice from murderers?" Monroe's eyes flicker to Richard. "That man isn't trustworthy. He sold his soul to the devil. His sexuality is an abomination against God—"

His temper flares hot and strident.

It curls within his entire body because *fuck* him. Richard is done living a lie. If he's fucking queer, then he'll damn well flaunt it.

"Let he be among us without sin and cast the first stone," Richard seethes. "If you have something to say, just say it to my fucking face."

"Now, I won't stand for any profanity—"

"I don't give a damn what you'll stand for," Richard snaps. "You're so damn quick to judge everyone else. You didn't give a damn about Beau when he needed help, and you sure as hell didn't give a damn about me when you found out I was queer—"

"I see the devil in you," Monroe says coolly. "Only the devil would justify his actions. You were just as bad as Mason, just as bad as those men that hurt and molested Beau, don't preach to me about judging. I am right to judge. As you will be (---), come the day my lord returns."

Richard swallows bitterly, hands shaking with unbridled fury.

He's not wrong. Monroe is right. Richard is bad, if not worse. He did unspeakable things and called it love. He kept Beau for himself instead of getting him therapy and guidance, and he tried to piss all over the system and tell them it was raining.

Richard takes responsibility for all his shortcomings, but being gay is something he will never apologize for. "You insolent fuck," he mutters darkly. "Maybelle could go to jail for years. A criminal record will ruin her whole life. She needs to tell Roy everything, or else her life will be over."

Monroe goes silent for several moments and then sighs deeply. "It's not her... it was my fault."

"What?" Roy demands.

"I... things had been slow; the recession had hit us hard. With this heatwave, my crops had all but dried up. The diner was barely turning a profit. I needed the funds quickly, and no bank could loan it to us, so I went to Neil."

"Neil Shaw?" Roy asks. "Where the hell did he get the money from?"

"I don't know, and I didn't ask." Monroe sits down heavily. "I am going bankrupt. The diner is all I have left... my wife... it was her mother's diner. It's been in the family for generations. I can't just sell it."

"So, you got in bed with a loan shark?" Richard asks, frowning.

"We all did," Monroe answers. "Someone is buying up all the property in Byrmonville, fast and furious. Neil might seem bad, but he isn't. He cares. He paid me the money; in exchange, I allow him to eat free at the diner. He warned me ahead of time about the Bandidos... some turf war... he said he would keep us out of it."

"How does Maybelle fit into all of this?" Roy asks.

"She made the deal for me... that's how they know her... sometimes my wife bakes cakes and cookies, she'll drop it off at the bar. I think that's how that Damian character was able to sink his claws into her."

"Damian hangs out there too?"

"Regularly, from what I heard."

"Shit." Roy shakes his head. "That means he's probably in bed with the Rebel Brotherhood, maybe he got into the wrong crowd, and that's what made him want to kill Casey—"

"They aren't bad men," Monroe chimes in.

Roy snorts. "Yeah, and I'm a monkey's uncle."

"I'm serious. I spoke with them, all of them. They're young men, most of them looking to live normal lives. I wouldn't lie to you. I have no reason to."

"Okay, suspension of disbelief aside, let's move on to the facts. Maybelle confessed to the murder, which makes her a prime suspect. Secondly, Damian confessed, which means he must be her accomplice. The question is, did they go there to kill Casey? And get scared last minute or did they kill her?"

"I think we all know the answer to that," Monroe responds. "My daughter isn't a killer. It's possible she didn't know they were being watched or followed."

"If you can get Maybelle to talk and give us some vital information, I'll remove those handcuffs myself. I promise." Roy reaches out to squeeze his arm.

"Thank you, son. I apologize for my words earlier... that's my baby girl." Monroe gets to his feet, worry lines creasing his forehead.

"I know... I have one at home too."

They laugh.

Richard sees red.

Roy pats Monroe on the back, steering him out of the office. The fucking bastard. It takes everything not to drive his fist straight into Roy's fucking face. Why is he even here? Richard scrubs his face, then leaves the room.

Several of the police officers surround Roy, speaking rapidly about the case. Richard looks across the hallway sadly, then walks out.

Who he is trying to fool? He doesn't belong here anymore.

CHAPTER 30

IT'S LATE BY THE time he leaves the station.

Richard realizes that it's after nine pm, and he's got several missed calls from an unknown number. Shit. Beau must have stopped by. Richard dials the number back, only for it to go straight to voicemail.

Fucking hell. Since Roy drove him to the station, he doesn't have a car. He'll have to walk the rest of the way home. Richard begins his journey, only to pause when he sees the large crowd at the bar across the street.

Men in leather jackets parade around amidst a sea of lights and smoke. He checks his phone again, realizing the unknown number texted him too.

Unknown 6:15 pm

It's me. I came by. U weren't there, so I left. I'm at the bar. Stop by if u want.

Richard pockets his phone, then walks over to the bar. The night seems alive. The air is so thick, it's almost as if he's underwater. The roar of the crowd and music thrums through his body. Sweat rains in the air, the women move hypnotically, their hips swaying to the heavy metal music pounding from the guitars.

A girl pushes into him, grinding her hips into his growing. "Dance with me."

"No thanks." Richard gives her a light shove, and she falls into the arms of someone else. He makes his way further inside. Several of the men are near the bar, their eyes are dark and cold.

Richard doesn't pay them any attention and makes his way to the back. He flicks back the curtains only to freeze when he sees Beau stepping out of his office.

"Hey," Beau says, approaching him slowly. He's got several papers in his hand, along with a beer. "I'm just finishing up. I'll be out soon."

"Sure," Richard replies, then smiles. He looks so different. Today Beau is wearing a simple white shirt. The sleeves are cut off, exposing his arms, a few new tattoos peek out here and there. "I'll wait at the bar?"

"Okay." Beau hesitates, then steps forward, placing a small kiss on his cheek.

Richard's face heats, his heart pounding in his chest. Beau turns around and disappears back into his office. The music is still blasting and there isn't anywhere to sit, so Richard leans against the wall near the bar.

His knee hurts. The pain moves from dull to pounding. He shouldn't have spent all day out at the station. The music doesn't help either.

"I'll be damned." Neil approaches him languidly, his voice carrying above the music. "Richard, isn't it?"

"Yeah." Richard looks at him coolly.

"The ex-sheriff of Byrmonville," Neil whistles. "Well, ain't that a cruel twist of irony."

Indeed. Richard tries to keep his expression neutral, but at the same time, he doesn't want to play games. Neil is a very dangerous man. He has no doubt that he's the one that killed Casey. The question is why?

Neil chuckles. It's loud and fake. Obnoxious. "Ain't you coppers all out to arrest us deviants? Now, look at you, one of us. It's ironic. The police officer is now on the other side."

"I guess." Richard shrugs dismissively. Already over the conversation.

"We all got our roles to play." Neil leers over him, grinning wildly.

"Yeah... and what's your role?" Richard asks. "How do you know Beau?"

"Now that's an interesting story," Neil responds. "I met Beau several years ago. He's a nomad like myself. See, I collect shards of broken things. Shiny sharp objects that I add to my shelf. Beau is the prettiest of them all. We held similar interests, a man after my own heart."

Richard bristles at that, jaw working. *So, they do have a relationship.*

His vision whirls. He can't share Beau. Not again. Not ever. Richard thought he made that clear. His stomach clenches like an empty soda can. He needs to get the hell out of here.

"Excuse me—"

"Now, don't mistake me." Neil laughs. "I ain't into that gay shit. I can appreciate a pretty face is all. No harm, no foul."

The bastard knew exactly what he was doing. Neil even said it in a way that insinuated they were lovers. Richard glares at him. "Then why did you phrase it like that—"

"Just wanted to confirm a few things is all." Neil lights a cigar, takes a long drag, and exhales. "Beau mentioned you, said you were someone important. I got curious."

Richard snorts, then looks away. *Fucker.*

"Your face is like a bulldog chewing a wasp." Neil shakes his head. "I see now how *special* you are. The truth is Beau owes me a debt. One he can never repay. Look around. These men aren't hardened criminals. They're the backwash, the rejects of society. We do what we do to survive. We're all intertwined. Don't worry. You'll see. Gentrification will come here as it does everywhere else. I gave Beau the torch, now it's up to him to set the world on fire."

"What do you want?"

Neil regards him for a moment. "To watch it all burn."

What the hell does that mean? Richard stares down at him, eyes narrowed. Who is this guy? Why does Beau keep him around?

"Ready?" Beau comes out from behind the curtains, his jacket thrown over his shoulder.

"Yeah, let's go."

~

Richard kisses Beau savagely.

Fisting his loose hair, shoving his tongue deep into his mouth. It's hot, a rush of sloppy hands and lips clashing together.

They stumble onto the bed. Richard runs his hands over the white shirt, marveling at the sinuous muscle beneath. Beau greedily undoes Richard's belt, peeling back the layers of his clothes. He tears off his pants, only to pause over the scar above his kneecap.

Beau carefully touches the raised skin, which is knotted pink. "How's the pain?"

Excruciating. "Okay."

His lip trembles, his hands shake around the lumpy white skin. "You—the cane... can you walk without it?"

"No."

There's no point in lying about it.

Beau crumples, eyes filling with tears as he gazes back at him. "Richard, I'm so sorry. It's my fault. I never meant for this to happen. I never—I'm so fucking sorry—"

"I never blamed you," Richard chimes in. "Not once." *I love you too much for that.*

"But—"

"I would do it all again. For you. For this. So that you could be free."

"I don't deserve it."

"You deserve everything," Richard says sternly.

Beau opens his mouth to say something, but Richard silences him with another kiss. He tugs the white shirt off Beau then removes his pants and socks. He takes his time, undressing him with sweet reverence.

CHAPTER 31

RICHARD TRAILS HIS HANDS down Beau's chest before following it with his mouth; with each soft gasp and sigh, the brightest hues burst across his vision.

It enters his soul.

Richard can't stop his hands from shaking. The pale flesh spreads out before him, tantalizing. He's drowning in a rainbow of colors and emotions.

"Richard," Beau breathes. He reaches into his pant pockets and hands him a condom and some lube.

There is a sudden burst of adrenaline, infused with built-up tension and imperishable need to consume Beau; he's so worked up he nearly came from the sight of it.

He grabs Beau's hips roughly, jerking his entire body toward him. The action is abrupt and makes Beau gasp loudly.

Richard leans in close and whispers like hot thunder, "I want you."

There isn't a point where Richard thinks to stop. The onslaught of emotions and the crazy haze of lust clouds his vision. He charges forward, melding their lips together in a brutish manner.

Beau is all hands and lips, barking curses and scratching wildly.

They slot together easily. By now, it comes as second nature and through thrusting hips and rapid cries. Beau is so smooth, beautiful, and flawless.

His eyes haunt south, following the minimal fine hairs down to Beau's resting pretty pink cock. He gasps, breath caught in his throat. Then spreads the lube over his fingertips.

"Spread your legs," Richard mumbles, his voice gruff and hoarse.

Beau's feline eyes studiously watch him.

There is a moment of hesitation before Beau complies, spreading his legs wider and observing his reaction. Richard groans, and his hands tremble forward, trailing up the alabaster thigh.

Using his sleek fingers, he pushes one ample cheek to the side before tracing the vernal, puckered entrance. It's all so mesmerizing, the feel of ridged skin against his rough thumb with the sound of the light hitch of Beau's breath.

Richard withdraws his hand, only to move toward his aching cock. Vanilla wraps around his throat, he chokes on it, before falling to his knees between Beau's thighs.

Spangled rows of fireworks dance before his eyes. A rush of passion consumes him, along with eternal fire. Richard's breath stutters, eyes widening as he makes exploratory circles around Beau's entrance with his fingers and then plunges in.

"Fuck." Beau bows, hands gripping the covers until his knuckles are white.

Everything is raging hot; Richard might burst into flames. Beau shudders beneath him, then tries to sit up.

"Lie down."

"You're hurt—let me—"

"It's alright." Richard pushes his chest lightly. "I'm okay."

"You're not—"

Richard leans back on his haunches, only for the pain to flare across his kneecap. His vision whites out, the ache spears across his knee and thigh. He grunts, twisting around and falling beside Beau, gripping his kneecap.

It's immeasurable. The agony judders across his bones, exploding into his heart. Beau scrambles, eyes wide with alarm. "Richard—are you okay?"

"Medication," he grits out. "In the bathroom." *Please.* Beau moves swiftly, running into the bathroom and grabbing what he can.

Richard chokes it down, face heating with embarrassment. It takes several moments, but finally, the pain subsides, and he takes a sip of water from a glass he keeps on his night table.

"Do you need anything else?" Beau asks, on his knees, holding his hand.

"No. I'm alright now."

Beau fixes him with a look of pure determination. "Lie down."

He pushes Richard back onto the bed. With one palm braced against his chest, Beau straddles him, holding him down as he pushes his ass against the hard length tenting Richard's boxers.

Beau bites his lip, rocking their hips together. His hair falls over his eyes. Richard reaches up, lets the strands trail through his fingers.

"Beau," Richard says through clenched teeth. Beau moves so maddeningly slow against him. The friction isn't nearly enough. Richard grabs a handful of Beau's hair and tugs. It earns him a quiet whimper.

"Stop teasing."

Beau ignores him. He whines when Richard grabs his hips and pushes up forcefully, letting his cock press between his ass cheeks through the thin layer of clothing.

"Let me fuck you."

"You're hurt." Beau looks down at him, pupils dark, already breathing hard from just this much. If Richard was in much better shape himself, well—that was entirely the fault of this ridiculous man in his bed. Richard smacks his ass. Beau grabs both his arms and pins them to his sides. "You're hurt. You need to rest."

"I don't care."

"I know you don't, but I do," Beau replies. He leans down, peeling off Richard's boxers, the last barrier between them. His hands quickly return to hold Richard's wrists, holding him still. "But I care. Won't you let me take care of you, just this once?"

Beau ducks down to kiss him suddenly before whispering against his lips, "Allow me, please."

Beau settles across his hips, reaching behind to prepare himself with lube, sliding the condom over Richard's aching cock.

Richard curls one hand around the back of his neck and drags him down until their mouths collide. Beau lets out a gasp—whether from the sting of teeth or his fingers, Richard doesn't know. What he knows is the warmth of Beau's mouth, the little sounds of pleasure and need that he wrings from those lips.

His free hand wanders down Beau's broad back.

Over the curve of his waist and the swell of his ass. His knuckles brush against Beau's slick fingers as they work into his tight hole.

"Ah, Richard, wait—" Beau shudders when Richard works his fingers into his entrance. "Wait. Don't do that."

"No?" Richard squeezes his ass instead. "You can usually take more than this."

"I can take whatever you're willing to give me," Beau whispers, resolute. Like he is stating a fact of nature. And Richard wants to laugh, wants to cry, because how can he ever give enough to replace everything that Beau has lost?

Chapter 32

Yet, Richard feels the angular jut of his hips, the firm planes of his chest. His cock is hard, pushing against Richard's stomach as Beau continues stretching himself.

"I can take it, but—" Beau bites his lip when Richard continues kneading his ass. "Let me do this for you. I just want to make you feel good today."

"You always do," Richard says quietly, and Beau pulls his fingers out and rises on his knees. His hands find their way to Beau's waist, gently positioning and guiding him.

Beau sinks on his cock.

The sudden breach of muscle, thick, sweltering, and tight, makes his throat go dry. Even with lube and preparation, it is a tight fit. Bit by agonizing bit, Beau takes every inch of him.

"Yes," he hisses. By now, he's delirious. Beau's face is pinched up, panting harshly as his hole stretches over the wide girth. The next slide is much more fluid, the muscle expanding instead of resisting, opening up, and sucking him in.

Beau braces his hands against the bed and begins to move.

Little motions at first, searching for the right angle, then steadily gaining speed and force until he practically impales himself on every downward stroke. Richard can't help canting his hips upward into that tight heat. The motion drives his cock deep into Beau, wrenching a loud moan from his lips.

Beau pants as Richard repeats the motion. "*Ahh.*"

Beau bites his lip to stifle another moan. Richard wants to pry his teeth open with his tongue, his fingers. He wants to memorize every sound Beau makes stretched around his cock. Wants to fuck him until Beau screams, until the only sound he knows is the shape of Richard's name in his mouth.

Richard lifts his knees and thrusts up hard, circling his arms around Beau's shoulders. Beau cries out, then crumples, whole body shaking from the vicious fucking.

I've got you. Richard holds him tightly while Beau makes muffled, trembling noises against his neck.

"Richard." His voice is barely audible. *"Ahhh*, fuck, I just want—"

A sob tears out of Beau's throat. Richard plunges his hips upward, far enough to drive Beau back down onto his cock. He captures his mouth in a desperate kiss, relishing the tears he feels against his face.

Beau's mouth spasms, breathing like he's been sliced open and ready to surrender. Richard groans loud and long as his cock plunges into deep, warm waters, and for the first time in months, he feels whole.

Everything after is easy; a series of hard, desperate thrusts that have him chasing the skyline.

The mingled smells of sweat and soap filled the air. Richard is a maniac, pounding brutally fast, gripping Beau's hips, bruising the tender skin.

Beau is practically sobbing with pleasure.

The numbness from before resolves as Richard finally comes to fruition, and it's damn near cosmological.

Sweat gathers on his back and lower brow. He sees luminous sparkles in the night, like someone had scattered Moondust and left it suspended above.

With a drunken cry of gratitude, he ascends, bypassing this world and flying onto the next.

When he comes it's like a catastrophic, vast explosion rippling through his entire body and momentarily paralyzing him. His cock keeps coming, gushing like a volcano as wave upon wave nearly drag him under.

Beau collapses onto him like a dead weight, his entire body quivering from the aftershocks.

~

"RICHARD?" Beau murmurs, blinking awake.

Bleary with sleep, squinting in the darkness, he reaches for Richard, who sits at the edge of the bed. Richard allows his hands to inch forward and catches his wrist. "Are you alright?"

"I'm fine. Go to sleep."

"Pain again?" Beau asks, sitting up.

Moonlight glows through the open windows, outlining Beau's serene face. Richard knows he'll never grow tired of looking at it.

"Something like that. Sleep."

Beau ignores him. "What time is it?"

"Just after midnight." Richard runs his thumb over the side of Beau's wrist, back and forth. "Go back to sleep."

He doesn't want to tell him the truth. That he can't think about losing him. It's unfathomable, inconceivable. That his cheeks are stained with tears, and his hands are shaking from the immeasurable force of his love.

In all ways, he's raw and beaten, bloodied and flailed by the weight of the demon. The responsibilities are heavy on his shoulders, yet all he wants is to remain here with Beau forever. How can he though? They've settled nothing. He knows nothing.

Beau is still an enigma, with thick walls and a deep well that keeps rebuilding as time passes. Who is this man? In his heart and his bed.

"Mm. Why are you awake?"

"Couldn't sleep."

"Need help?" Beau smirks wickedly, trailing his fingers up his arm.

Twice already he's lost this impossible man. Richard knows he cannot suffer a third time. Not when his heart is so full to bursting. He holds onto him as if he were a man in the desert dying of thirst chancing upon the water.

A hallucination of an oasis.

The mirage is so real, so tangible it curls within his gut as he takes hold of Beau again. This illusion, whether it's real or fake, he doesn't care. He never did.

Beau is his. Until the very end.

Chapter 33

All good things come to an end.

Richard knows that. Nothing in this world lasts forever. Even here and now. He doesn't want to waste what little time he's got left on beating around the bush. The time to act is now.

Beau sits across from him at the table, reading the newspaper and eating cereal. It's been two days of straight fucking.

Richard knows his time is up. Reality will settle in. Then he'll have to face the consequences of his actions, and he'd rather do that now than later.

"We need to talk."

The words come out halting, his baritone voice echoing in the tiny space between them. Beau looks up from the paper, eyes wide and startled.

He left this morning to handle something at work, returning a few hours later with a backpack full of clothing. Richard didn't question it, yet it lit up his soul, and he kissed Beau until they were both breathless.

It's what he wants. Desperately.

He wants Beau to live with him forever. To consume his world and never leave. Yet, for that to happen, he needs to know the truth. No matter of ugly it is.

"Sure." Beau gives his full attention. "What do you need? I reckon this is about Neil."

"Yes." Richard's throat clogs, but he's determined to get this out. "And about *before*..."

"Before?"

"With Mason... I don't want to know the details... I just want to know... if... was it real? Did you love me at all or—"

He can't speak. The anguish threatens to strangle him alive. Did Beau ever care, or was it all about killing Gary and Mason? Did he set him up for the fall on purpose? Or did things just happen that way?

"It was real," Beau says strongly. He reaches across the table to take his hand. "It was always real."

"Then..." Why?

Beau looks away, emerald eyes darting rapidly across the table top. "It *was* real... but at first, it wasn't. At least not for me."

When that man fucked me... I didn't know... I didn't know... it could feel so good. Sex for Beau meant something entirely different.

Richard remembers vividly the way his stomach roiled from even the thought. Beau enjoyed sex with many men, relished in it even.

That I needed to be fucked and I craved it, in the worst way possible. It was so twisted and wrong; Richard recalls being filled with contemptuous rage. At times Beau often confused rape and molestation for affection, at some points citing that Mason cared for him.

They cared for me, they touched me and loved me way more than my daddy ever did, and when they fucked me... I have not felt anything like it—every single time. I need it, Richard. I need it to live. Like air, like breathing air.

Like air. Even now, he's revolted. The words haunt him as he thinks back to that faithful day. Where does Neil fall into this? Is he another

Mason or Enos? Taking advantage of Beau and leaving him in the gutter.

He won't allow it. Not now or ever.

"I... understand." It hurts. So very badly.

From the moment he saw Beau, he loved him. Although, he won't proclaim his innocence. At first, Richard used him to fulfill his sexual gratification because he was too scared to come out. To be himself.

He'll forever regret that.

What? Men like you? Who treats me like nothing but a nice, comfy hole for their cocks? Yes, indeed, Richard was no different.

"You were just another John... plus I didn't want to spend another night in jail... Mason would be furious, and I saw the way you looked at me..." Beau mutters. "So... at first... it was nothing to me. Sex. Money. You paid very well, and you were consistent... but after Mason died... I ... I was so fucking angry... nobody cared... I wanted the fucker dead," Beau utters, hands clenching at his side.

Something in his expression switches. It's quick and strident, like lightning. The docile creature before him transforms, face hardening into fury.

"This whole town is shit. I was abused for years. Nobody cared. Not even the fucking *sheriff*. How many times did the police call my daddy and Creed? Nothing happened. I was the local prostitute everybody knew about but didn't lift a goddamn finger to help! It's only when I started sucking your cock that they finally gave a fuck! By then, it was too late!"

Beau rages, eyes blazing at him. "By then, I'd already stabbed the fuck out of Gary! Everyone thought he was a saint! Nobody knew how he tortured me! Or ripped apart the skin off my back!"

He stands, jaw working angrily. "I'm a worthless piece of trailer park trash. Nobody cared if I lived or died."

Richard is helpless.

He watches the storm brew until it charges toward him. Beau is furious, panting wildly as he gazes down at Richard with hatred simmering in his bones.

Nobody cared.

"Creed only came back because the cartels were after him. He only cared about his money! The bastard didn't give a fuck if I was raped and brutalized for the rest of my goddamn life—" Beau violently kicks over his chair, fuming like mad. "I could kill the bastard again. The worthless cunt who *used* me to do everything! I could kill them all! I *want* them all to burn, Richard!"

His voice is so loud, so thunderous.

Richard shrinks back. He's a different person. Filled to the brim with cavernous malevolence. His eyes warp, turning into miserable, angry black slits.

CHAPTER 34

"BEAU," RICHARD SAYS SOFTLY. "I'm sorry. We failed you. I failed you."

Beau throws his head back and laughs. He laughs so hard, and for so long, he cries. He crumples to his knees, gripping onto Richard's pants as if they are his lifeline.

"And then you came. A dumb sheriff who asked me if I ate properly... if I slept properly... if anything was wrong. Richard Clayson. Married. Handsome. You cared. Even when I forgot how to." He releases a shuddering breath. "I hated you for it. For caring. For asking. Nobody ever asked, and you did. I wanted you gone, and I didn't care how or when.

"Then—" He's trembling, fisting his jeans, tears trailing down his cheeks. "—*then* you said you loved me. *Nobody loves me*. Not even my own—" A sob rips through his throat. "Not even my brother loved me, but you did. And it *was* real. I couldn't believe it."

Beau gasps, teeth clenching around endless tears. "I didn't believe it, so I let Enos suck me off. I convinced myself it wasn't real. I fucked you over because I told myself you would leave anyway. I hated you. Everyone knew you had the perfect wife. The perfect family. I tore us apart because I *wanted* to."

Richard lets the words pierce his heart.

Lets them run straight through his chest until his eyes brim with his tears. Yes, he's had his suspicions for a long time. No act of God or Satan could've removed Beau from his life unless he did it of his own volition.

"It wasn't until after I tore us apart… *after* I told you I never loved you that I realized I did. I do. I never stopped. I can't stop. You love me, and I love you. *God*—" Beau wrenches forward. "I am such a coward, Richard. I've done unspeakable things to you—I've crippled you. You can barely walk because of me. Your life is destroyed because of me—" He releases an agonizing wail. "I hate myself for it—"

"*Don't*," Richard barks at him, bitter tears sliding down his cheeks. He grabs Beau's forearms and yanks him into his arms. "Don't ever say that. You were so young. It was my fault. I took advantage of you. I shouldn't have—I should be the one begging your forgiveness."

Beau quivers in his arms. "I wanted you. I still do. You love me. I love you so much, Richard. These years apart have been hell. I can't be away from you anymore. Don't turn me away from your life. I can't stand it. I can't—I won't."

Richard nods frantically, fisting Beau's hair. "You are my life. I swear it. We will be together. I love you too."

Beau cries harder then, allowing the weight of everything to come down finally.

Richard can do nothing but wait, allow the snow plains to crush him underneath a violent blizzard. Beau hangs onto him, knuckles white and body heaving from his cries.

His sorrow runs bone-deep.

The kind that can never be healed. Richard will wait, patience among the withering decay, the flower amidst the storm.

He'll wait four seasons. Ten. A lifetime and more.

"Neil is nothing to me," Beau whispers urgently. "A mongoose among the snakes. He taught me everything I know about the business. We're partners. Nothing more. There is only you. There's never been anyone else."

"Okay." Richard releases a hard breath. *Okay*.

Beau's hands sprawl all over him, like an octopus, he coils around him tightly. "I love you."

Richard lets out a wet laugh, cradling Beau's face. "I love you too."

He claims his lips roughly, forcing his tongue into Beau's mouth. Richard kisses his cheeks, tasting the salty sweetness of tears and sweat on his skin, biting and licking his way down to Beau's neck, sucking a bruise into his collarbone.

This is it.

This is what it feels like to be whole. Ever since he lost Beau, he's always felt he's missing one half, unbalanced, and off-kilter. Like a table with three legs.

We are the same—you and I, Mason had said. Things are different now. Beau is old enough to make his own decisions. They won't be hiding in secret. Of fear of being caught by the police or his wife. They finally have a chance to live out in the open now.

As a real couple.

"Take me to bed," Beau breathes against his lips. "*Please*."

Yes, God, yes. Beau breathes shallowly while Richard kisses his forehead, his cheeks. With his large thumb, he wipes away the evidence of tears.

Richard stands, lifting Beau into his arms. Beau's legs automatically wrap around his narrow waist. He lays Beau onto the bed, unwraps him like a Christmas gift, one layer at a time.

Beau's lashes glisten with tears. He whimpers when Richard enters him, slow and deep, trying to combine their souls. He bottoms out inside Beau, and a fresh wave of tears overcome him.

Richard melds their bodies together, burying his face in the crook of Beau's neck. Heat curls in his gut, along with everlasting protectiveness and trust.

"It's okay," Richard murmurs, moving inside of him. "I'm here. I've got you."

With his eyes shut, Beau fumbles for his hand under the blankets, gripping it with a fierceness that stings. And Richard grips his hand right back.

Richard folds over him, encasing his love in a cocoon.

The demon settles within, soothing away sadness and kissing each scar Beau tried to hide from others. It's rare. The soft side of this lonesome creature.

Beau, the brilliant soul that he is, finds love and solace in the demon's embrace.

CHAPTER 35

THE MORNING COMES AS a promise kept.

Richard basks in its radiance, drawing Beau closer to his chest. A perfect fit, a missing puzzle piece. He sighs deeply, tasting the remnants of yesterday's tears, the grief that seems to settle like winter ice in his bones.

It's beginning to thaw. Not yet, but slowly, surely.

He reaches over to check his phone, frowning when he sees five missed calls from Roy. "Shit," he mumbles, untangling himself from Beau.

The last thing he needs is for Roy to get worried and show up at his doorstep. Richard dials the number, shrugging on his t-shirt and some shorts.

"Roy Rhett."

"It's me."

"Where the fuck have you been?" Roy snarls. "I've been trying to reach you."

Richard closes the bedroom door. "I'm sorry... I've been... *busy*..."

Roy snorts a laugh. "Whatever. Look, there's a problem at Kyle's school. Turns out he got into a fight with one of the boys. Broke his nose or some shit, and I can't get away from the office. Lana started her job yesterday in Gainesville—"

"I'll get him."

"You sure?" Roy asks.

Richard's blood boils. "He's still my son."

"Just asking, brother," Roy placates. "Isaac—bring me those files. I want to go over them—alright. You can bring him to the house, and I'll try to get off work as soon as possible. Ida is in school then after school care until five, you know, the one on Keller Street—"

"I remember."

"Right."

There's an awkward silence. Roy starts shuffling papers, mumbling to himself, and Richard tries to calm down. "I'll pick him up now. Talk to you later."

"Okay, take care."

Richard hangs up. *Jackass.*

Walking back inside the bedroom, he sits down on the bed and scrubs his face. He needs to shower. Then he'll go pick up Kyle from school. "Hey." He leans down, brushing the hair away from Beau's forehead. "Are you okay?"

"Mhmm," Beau hums but doesn't open his eyes.

"I'm going to pick up Kyle and drop him home. I'll be back soon."

"Okay."

"Love you." He presses a kiss to his cheek, savoring the feel of plush skin. Richard gets ready, showering and then taking his medication for the day. It's after eleven by the time he leaves. The morning air is crisp and clean, the grass still wet with dew.

He stops by a coffee shop he knows Kyle used to love and gets their usual order. Richard allows the nervousness to engulf him. After all, it's been a few weeks since they last saw each other.

So much has happened. Richard doesn't want to risk becoming estranged from his son. It would devastate him too much. Without further delay, he pulls into the parking lot. The school knows he's coming. He called ahead of time to make sure that Kyle would be ready for pick up.

Richard steps out of his vehicle, cane firmly in his grasp as he walks with measured steps toward the principal's office. The secretary's eyes widen when she sees him, and she jumps up from her desk. "Richard? Is that you?"

"Hey, Martha." Richard nods. "How're you?"

"I'll be damned," she drawls. "You look... good... all things considering."

Small town. "Thank you."

Martha steps around her desk, her round face morphing into concern. "We heard about... everything really... Patrick, he can't be around that... I hope you understand..."

Right. Patrick had been Kyle's best friend. It seems they aren't anything anymore. Richard doesn't respond because there's nothing to say. He killed a man in cold blood, fucked a prostitute, and got fired all in six months.

What parent would *want* their child around that?

She steps forward timidly, hands clasped together. Her face softens; chubby cheeks make her look younger. "I'm sorry. I wish—you and Lana have been so good to me, especially after Patrick's father ran off. I did everything I could to support Lana—"

"I understand. Is Kyle ready?"

Martha nods. "Yeah... he's in the back."

"Thanks." Richard walks past her and knocks on the door. "Kyle? It's me."

Kyle rips open the door, glaring daggers up at him. "Let's go."

Richard nods quietly. He thanks Martha one last time before they leave the school. The walk to the car is quiet. Kyle is steaming mad as they both get into his truck. He takes several deep breaths and gets into the front seat but doesn't start the vehicle.

"Kyle..."

"I said let's go. I want to go home."

Richard turns to him, frowning deeply. He's let this go on long enough. Yes, he's done horrible things. He deserved everything that he got. He'll never dispute that, but Kyle is his son, and he should show him more respect. "What happened?"

"Nothing," he mutters, turning his face away. Richard notices the faint bruises on his cheek and brow and the scratches on his arm.

"You've been fighting."

"Me?" he exclaims. "I never do anything. They make fun of me all the time."

"Kyle—"

"I know what you're going to say. That I should let it slide. That it's only words, but it's not. They say you never loved Mom and that you're a-a-a queer. I asked Roy and Mom about it, and they said it was a lie. It's not true. You loved Mom. Everything will go back to normal. It has to."

Richard swallows thickly. "I'm sorry, buddy."

"No. I've been good. I've been good," he cries, pounding his fist against the dashboard. "I-If I am good, you'll come home, and things will go back to the way they were. You loved Mom. I know you did. You aren't... what they're calling you."

Blood roars in his ears. Richard's hands shake as the words wash over him. It's true. All of it. Richard should never have let things go on for so long. It's so sick and wrong.

He's a bastard for doing this to Kyle. For lying to him.

"I am."

Kyle turns to him, eyes wide and wet.

"Gay," he continues, slow and steady. "I lied to your mom about it. I lied to you about it. I'm sorry."

Kyle looks away, eyes searching, trying to understand. "You like men more than women?"

"Yes." Richard takes his hand. "But that doesn't mean I don't have room for all of you. I love you all. So much. I don't love anyone more or less."

"What about Beau?" Kyle demands. "It always seems like you love him the most."

Richard sighs. "I don't. I love you all equally. I'm just bad at distributing my love. I just need more time with you. That's all. You're my son. I love you."

"Oh." Kyle looks at his hands. "In school... they said it's okay... to love men, I mean... Just some kids are so stupid. It doesn't make any sense to me."

"Me neither... They make fun of me too... but it doesn't change my feelings for you. I never stopped loving you. What I did was wrong, Kyle. Killing people is wrong. Taking someone against their will is wrong. I want you to know that, but being gay isn't wrong."

Kyle goes quiet, chewing his bottom lip. "I see."

"I'll take you home." Richard pats his hand and starts the car. The rest of the ride, he's deep in thought, trying to figure out a way to salvage the situation before it's too late. "Do you want to hear a joke?"

Kyle perks up immediately.

"Why did the teddy bear say no to dessert?"

Kyle thinks about it for a moment, then shrugs.

"Because she was stuffed."

Kyle gives him a deadpan look. "Weak, Dad. So very weak."

"You got something better?"

"What is brown, hairy, and wears sunglasses?"

"Mhm, what?"

"A coconut on vacation."

Richard snorts, shaking his head. "Is that the best you can do? I thought I taught you better than that."

"No, wait, that was a test one!"

"Who says?" Richard demands in faux outrage. "If yours was a test, so was mine. It's only fair!"

Kyle burst out laughing. "No! I mean it. I've got another one. It wasn't even my best."

Chapter 36

Time passes.

Weeks wane in the sleepy town of Byrmonville. Richard soaks in it. The moments with Beau are like a warm bath, fragrant, decadent. He lingers there peacefully.

Beau sweeps into his life with fluidity and grace, immersing himself between every crease and crevice. It's an unspoken agreement. A toothbrush here, a hair tie there, clothing stuffed into drawers, and razors left out on the sink counter.

He moves in.

Slowly, languidly. Like the time and space between them never existed at all. Bills are mysteriously paid for; the fridge is always stocked. Richard is happier than ever. To have his lover with him again makes his blood sing.

They make love during the day. Heat and sweat cling to their skin in a film of perspiration. Richard marks every part, every inch of Beau's endless skin. The demon wants to kill and destroy, to suffocate his lover by ripping out their jugular.

Yet, it still marvels at his lover's brittle bones. It's too much. Richard stares at his pretty erect nipples, swollen with abuse by his broad ivory teeth.

Beau's mouth looks almost painted, rich hues of red and pink flood his cheeks. He brims with a diabolical glow, so seductive and salacious. Richard beams with the realization that it's because of him.

Afterward, basking in the healthy radiance of copious fucking, Beau dresses for work. Richard lies on his back, stroking his stomach, his cock spent and flaccid. "What time will you be back?"

Beau smirks. "Soon."

Then he's gone. Richard watches him leave, heart inflating, practically bursting at the seams. Later on, he gets dressed, throwing on a pair of old jeans and some cowboy boots he found in his closet. It's a nice day. The air is breezy and filled with a summer haze.

Some fresh air might be good.

Richard steps outside, and glances around. He takes several steps before he's swarmed. The sirens blare as two police cruisers pull up to his doorstep.

Roy steps out of the car, aviator glasses on.

This isn't a social call. Richard's stomach drops, hands clenched at his side.

Roy looks away, jaw working. Two cruisers. It means he's their primary suspect. Richard sighs and walks toward one of the cruisers.

It's humiliating, degrading even.

"Can I at least get my cane?" His voice is small, broken. There's nothing left to fight for anyway.

"I'll get it," Roy says gruffly, then goes inside his apartment. Several moments later, he comes out with the cane and hands it to Isaac, then he holds the car door open, and Richard slinks inside.

The ride to the station is very short. Richard takes his time walking through the halls. Tanya and Hiromi avert their eyes, and Houston gives him a pitying look.

Just as well. Richard is tired of this too.

They lead him to the interrogation room and force him to sit down. Richard's mind races, every muscle locked in place. Tanya sits down across from him, hands clasped on the table.

He remembers when he trained her. Still fresh out of the academy, a ball of nervous energy as their first preparatory hurled racist insults at her. She took it all in stride; she never even flinched.

They arrested the bastard on drug charges two days later. It hurts to know that he'll be treated the same. Roy enters after several minutes with Hiromi on his heels, they all take a seat across from him.

"State your name," Tanya says.

"Richard Clayson."

She asks some more general questions, and then they get right down to it.

"Am I under arrest?"

"No," Roy injects quickly. "We just need some clarification, is all."

His brain stutters for a moment. He blinks rapidly, eyes taking in more light than expected. Everything pauses when he struggles to catch up: Richard is doused with cold water, heat pulsating from the shock of being brought into the office in such a manner.

"Why didn't you just call?"

"Formalities." Roy waves his hand dismissively, but it's a lot more than that. Whatever Richard says, Roy wants it on record. "Plus, you're still considered a flight risk, you were just released from state prison. I didn't want to take any chances."

That makes no sense. Unless Roy just wanted to humiliate him.

"I see," Richard replies. "Then what can I do to help?"

Roy shoves some photos in front of him. They're surveillance photos of Maybelle at the precinct several hours before the time of the murder. "It seems she was there. The cameras picked her up near the back. If you look through them, she's pacing back and forth almost as if she's waiting for someone."

Shit. "Did she give a reason why she was there?"

"No, she's not talking. Keep looking. It gets better."

Richard flips through the pictures, and his eyes widen when he sees Damian show up several moments later. Maybelle leaves at the back door, and then Damian enters, almost as if he's following after her.

Their behavior is so bizarre. Damian paces back and forth too, then whips around and leaves in the other direction, opposite Maybelle. *What the fuck?*

They were there, both of them. This puts the smoking gun in their hands.

CHAPTER 37

"ANY FORMAL ARREST MADE?"

"Not yet, brother," Roy injects. "We're still looking for a missing piece, but we're close. Turns out Damian does some part-time work downtown at a paint shop. They noticed some of their materials missing, all we need to do is match the handwriting, and with his full confession, we can have him convicted."

"Then why are you hesitating?"

"Some things are not adding up," Hiromi says. "First off, why confess to the murder? Then vehemently retract your statement? Casey was his mother and his only ally. Without her, the rape charges against him would probably have him thrown away in federal prison. Why kill her? Because she refused one case? Maybelle is another question mark. Her motive is flimsy at best. I know her. She's a good girl. It's going to be hard to convict her when half the town knows her."

"You think they're being set up," Richard concludes. It's a good assessment. "By who?"

"Exactly," Roy chimes in. "I think it's bigger than Casey and everything else going on. Remember what Monroe said? About some new guy buying up all the property in Brymonville. Well, guess what? The fucker bought the grocery store on the ninth avenue, they're doing a bunch of renovations, and do you know who I saw there? Fucking

Neil Shaw! The bastard was putting up drywall with the rest of his crew."

Richard's throat goes dry.

The room narrows down, and he can barely breathe past the roaring in his head. Their fridge is always stocked. He never questioned where the food came from. It all made sense now. That's where all the money was going, into buying real estate.

"I see..."

"We know Maybelle's connections to Neil are through Monroe and the money he owes them, but what about Damian? Where does he fall into everything? So, we did some digging. Turns out he's addicted to cocaine. He was going through withdrawal at the time of his confession. He's getting treatment for it, but his only supplier is the Rebel Brotherhood."

If Neil withheld drugs to get Damian to kill Casey, then that would be his motive to kill her, but it's still a stretch. "It's too circumstantial."

"You think so?" Tanya asks.

"I agree..." Hiromi responds. "For starters, what would Neil have against Casey? They didn't know each other. Casey was going to reopen the investigation against Blackwell... Not Neil. Why would he want her dead?"

"Perhaps their lovers," Roy says darkly, eyes flickering to Richards.

Richard glares at him. "What the fuck is that supposed to mean?"

"I mean... no offense... Beau always got around... perhaps... Neil is doing his lover a favor."

Anger curls hot and unstoppable in his gut. A lie. Too vicious to ever be repeated.

Richard clenches his hands tightly.

This is exactly what Roy wants. The bastard is fucking fishing, *again*. This time with witnesses around. He wants to know exactly where he falls into the scheme of things. It's a double-edged sword. If he defends Beau, then he's automatically siding with the Rebel Brotherhood and becomes their primary suspect. If he says nothing, then he's withholding information.

Richard feels his temper rising. It bustles hot in his veins as he struggles to control the blinding rage. *Goddamn him.*

There's no way around this. Out of everyone in Byrmonville, Beau Blackwell would gain the most from Casey's death.

And Roy damn well knows it.

Richard's got nothing to lose. He's wasted too much time in the shadows. The clock is ticking, time is running out, and soon he'll be gone.

"They're not lovers."

"Now, don't take offense, brother," Roy placates, chuckling softly. "I'm just speculating here, but though the process of elimination it just makes sense, you know—"

"They're *not* lovers," Richard grits out.

The laughing stops immediately, Roy's expression transforms, smile slowly fading from his lips. "Richard—you didn't tell me—you promised me—"

"I did," Richard barks ruthlessly. "I am. Beau cannot be Neil's lover. He's already mine."

~

"FUCK. I should have known better."

Roy tips his head back, looking up at the sky. It's tinted sepia, wheatgrass bathed in orange, and the sky a velvet carpet, calling to the souls of nighttime.

"I should be pissed, but I'm not surprised. Not at all. I kind of expected it."

Richard doesn't respond. He looks out into the distance, wishing he could fall into the abyss.

"You've been different recently... happier I think..." Roy continues. "I thought it's because you and Kyle patched things up... I just... *fuck*... Lana isn't going to take this well."

"Let me tell her," Richard replies. "I need to be the one."

"You know I never cared about that gay shit, right?" Roy chucks his cane into the field. "It's just Beau—he twists you up inside—got you all backward and shit. It ain't right. He's only been back a few months, and it's like he's already dragging you into his shit."

"I know."

Richard isn't blind. He willfully goes, head first.

"You love him?" Roy demands.

"I never stopped."

"Then you're a fool." Roy turns away from him, shaking his head. "A damn fool." He opens his cruiser door. "Come on. I'll take you home."

They pull up in front of his apartment building. Roy kills the engine, then rubs the back of his neck. "I ain't ever been good with words, but I do want you to be happy, Richard... it kills me... every day lying to Lana and the kids. You should tell them. They deserve to know about your—"

"There's no point. I want to enjoy the time I have with them," Richard cuts him off and then opens the car door. "I'll keep you posted if I hear or see anything suspicious."

Roy gives him a hard look. "See that you do."

CHAPTER 38

Sunshine hits his scales at an angle.

Its colossal form is like chunks of smooth crystals, refracting and reflecting the light. Endless mist of the early morning cascades around them. Richard leans in, kissing those petal-soft lips again and again.

What is skin compared to scales or bone to horns?

Rising embers and smoke, a scythe-like tail rattling behind them. Richard awakes in his true form, bright light dancing on the tips of his yellow slit eyes.

A creature with prey locked in his arms.

"I have to go—" Beau says between kisses, his meaty thighs mounted on his bike. It's early. Too early. "They need me—"

"I do too." Richard covers his lips again. "Call in sick."

Beau chuckles. "I can't—"

"But you're the boss," Richards groans, then relents, pulling away. "Fine."

"I'll be back soon." Beau smiles, hair mused. "I promise."

Richard cups his cheeks then looks down at the Harley Davidson. It's a nice bike. Expensive. Surely not something just anyone can afford. He takes in the sleek pipes, steel and shining, and notes several stains on the seats. "What's this?" He touches it. "Looks like dried paint?"

"Some renovation at the shop," Beau explains. "I didn't have time to clean it off."

Odd.

Richard doesn't comment on it. Or the fact that the paint looks like it's been there for several weeks. Since the auto shop was fairly new, they could have been redoing one of the rooms. It's plausible. Believable.

Yet, something like doubt coils in him. Richard stuffs it down, sealing his lips over Beau's in quick succession. "When will you be back?"

"I haven't even left." Beau puffs a laugh. "Soon. After five maybe? It's too hot. I can't work in this heat."

"Okay..." Richard hesitates. "Listen... I told Roy... about us... and I want Lana to know too, along with my kids."

Beau looks away, staring off into the sunrise. "Are you sure? After everything... I figured they probably hate me."

They do. "I... I want you in my life. I need you there. They'll just have to get over it."

"I don't know, Richard." Beau looks at the ground. "Lana's never liked me and Roy... well, he's always been suspicious of me. I don't know if it's worth ringing up trouble—"

"It's no trouble," Richard says sternly. "I love you. We're together. Nothing troubling or shameful about that."

"If you're sure," Beau responds. "I'll follow your lead."

Richard beams at that.

"Now I do have to go," Beau says, then kisses him sweetly. "I'll text you later."

Then he's off, in a sea of black smoke, with the engine thundering. Heat spreads along his chest as he smiles softly to himself. It's strange, nameless, filling him with warmth and devotion.

It's several hours later he realizes what it was.

It's hope.

~

"I KNOW."

Richard grips the phone tightly, hands shaking around the receiver. It's no guess who told her, and judging by her tone, she isn't at all happy.

"Look, I ain't—the kids are still my priority. I want to see them as often as I can, and I promise you—"

"I told you I needed time."

"Lana—"

"I need time, Richard," she says. "You can't just... spring this on us... we're barely scraping by as it is. I am happy you're happy, but the kids are adjusting to Roy as their new normal, and now this? I don't know."

Richard bristles. "Now what?"

"Now you want them to get to know someone else? Someone who may not stick around—"

"What the hell is that supposed to mean?"

"Someone with a questionable past—"

"Not by choice."

"He was a *child*, Richard," Lana whispers furiously. "He was a child. You took advantage of a child. If that had happened to Kyle." Her voice breaks off into a sob. "Or Ida... God, I can't even bear the thought of it. *He loves you; you love him*. I get it. Now that he's a consenting adult, you want to *parade* your relationship around like it was just and good. He depended on you. He had no one else. It was wrong. You did time in prison for him. You've atoned for your mistakes. Has he? Has Beau sought any kind of counseling? Has he gotten help for the years of abuse? Ask yourself *that*, Richard. Is he truly, okay?"

Richard's stomach roils.

The air is knocked out of his lungs as his legs turn to water. It's ugly. His reflection. For years he thought they were homophobic. Maybe they were, maybe they still are, yet it goes far deeper than that.

To them, Richard will always be in the wrong. No matter how much older Beau is. He manipulated him. Richard is the monster here.

And it kills him.

"I..." He is speechless. What more is there left to say? *I love him, and I can't leave him.* It's too selfish. Too profane.

Lana is right. If he cared, he'd look into counseling. Something—anything to get Beau the mental health help he needs. He tried before, and Beau vehemently refused.

"You're right. I'm sorry."

"I'm not saying never. You can bring him around. I'm not against *that*... just let the dust settle. Make sure he's here for good. Kyle already knows he's in town... he's looking forward to seeing him again... but things need to be different this time, Richard. Solid."

"Of course."

"I need full disclosure from you... at all times. We're a family. I want to include Beau as well... but it needs to be done the right way. Gradually."

Richard's mouth fills with cotton.

His airways close, his throat dries, and his tongue swells. It's all so dreadful. How could he have overlooked so much? Beau isn't a thing to be kept and swaddled. He's a person. A human.

He needs to do better. For Beau and himself.

"Thank you."

"No problem. I look forward to getting to know him, properly this time. Things will work out, Richard. I promise."

Lana is right.

They've been living in a dreamland. Eventually, things will crumble. Is Richard willing to uphold this mirage? Defend it until his last breath or can he forge his way?

Push through until they both come out on the other end. What choice does he have?

When the only way out is the way through.

CHAPTER 39

BEAU EMERGES FROM THE water, tight red shorts clinging to his thighs.

It's obscene. The filmy piece of fabric he calls a bathing suit. Richard scoffs at it, knowing he'll soon be tearing it off with his teeth.

Beau plops down beside him, hair plastered to his forehead and neck, water dripping down his chest. He towels his hair dry and smiles when Richard hands him a beer.

"Thanks," he says, taking a long sip.

Fins for limbs, born of the ocean. Demons often linger in the caverns, the darkest holes, and the deepest pits, where no light can penetrate. Richard can easily shift, turn water into the air and move as easily within the sky as he does the sea.

"You going in?" Beau asks, turning to look at him.

It's a sunny day. The place is secluded, hidden behind a grotto of forest and foliage. Their lagoon is a timeless place.

"Not today."

He wouldn't say he awoke in agony this morning.

His knee flares with fire so hot he cupped his mouth to withhold a scream. It morphed into an ear-splitting headache that left him whimpering on the bathroom floor for hours.

Although his otherworldly form can slice through water like paper, his human form cannot. He's bound to this world, destined to weave into the next.

He's almost out of time.

Richard's stomach clenches, rising nausea settles over him. It's good to be here. At least one last time. "I'll dip my feet in."

Beau looks at him skeptically. They sit in silence for a while. Their bodies close together. Richard takes out some sandwiches he packed, along with some iced tea. He eats slowly, taking his time to savor each bite.

"Motorcycle accident."

Richard turns to Beau inquisitively.

"That's how Creed died."

Oh.

Richard stares back at his iced tea. He's never particularly liked Creed. The junkie bastard always treated Beau like shit. He hated him before, and he still hates him now. "I'm sorry to hear that."

He's not. He's glad, actually.

Beau snorts, hands clenching around the beer bottle. "Bastard pissed everyone off. I'm surprised he lasted this long. Fucker died drowning in his blood."

A motorcycle accident? How strange. "Did they do an autopsy?"

"Sure did. The idiot was so high he drove right into a steel pole. It's a lie, though. Creed was always high. He drove high all the time. Neil's got this theory that the cartels caught up to him and ran him off the road."

"I see."

"Everybody leaves," Beau mutters. "Nobody sticks around. I thought I'd be happy, you know? He always forced me into prostitution. Making me fuck his friends and shit. I thought, great, the bastard's dead, finally. Then I realized I was the last one left. The last Blackwell in history."

Richard listens intently. It must have been a horrible shock to find out everyone in your family is dead.

"I... I didn't know what to do... where to go... with the money Creed stole, we were the only two people that knew where it was. So... I told Neil... he taught me what to do with it. We tripled it and then kept moving from town to town to avoid suspicion."

A nomad, like myself, Neil had said.

"I... I wanted to make something of myself. To be something more. I have always liked math and numbers. It came naturally to me, more than words and shit. So... Neil... helped me get my GED. He enrolled me in school, taught me about finances and running a business... kept me safe... never judged me or forced me to sleep with anyone... I owe him a lot."

It feels like a punch to the stomach.

The iced tea turns sour in his mouth. It curdles, turning vinegarish sludge on his tongue. *Beau did all of that without him.*

It stings.

To know that Beau accomplished everything and more with someone else. Richard should be glad, he should congratulate Beau on all of it, but he can't.

The words clog his throat.

He spent weeks trying to get him to school to convince him he was more than a prostitute. It had taken everything to enroll him into the local high school, only for Beau to drop out after an encounter with Enos.

Richard did everything. Yet, still, Beau went elsewhere. A wave of bitterness sweeps over him, and he drinks his tea in silence. He can't change the past.

Beau is happy now. Successful. Well beyond his wildest dreams. Richard takes a deep breath, hands shaking, and turns to look at him. "I'm proud of you."

He means it.

"You've done such amazing things. I know before... it wouldn't have worked out. High school after Mason and Gary's deaths would have probably been impossible for you. I was wrong to force it... but I am glad, you were able to finish."

Richard resigns with the knowledge that Beau is content with his new life, even if Richard had no part of it. How could he? Especially since he spent four years in prison for killing Mason.

It's better this way.

"I did it for you," Beau blurts out.

Richard frowns. "What?"

"I did it all for you." Beau gets on his knees, eyes brimming with tears. "I wanted to make you proud. I wanted to be someone you could be proud of, to be worthy of you, Richard."

He pulls Beau into his arms, crushing his body to his chest. He's still wet, and the water soaks his shirt and pants. "Stop." Richard can't stand it. "You're always worthy of me. The question is, am I worthy of you?"

"I never forgot you. I always thought of you. Everyday. I swore I'd come back, no matter what. I'm so happy, Richard. I am so happy. We can finally be together forever."

Richard shudders.

Beau kisses him sweetly, tasting of minerals and salt. It's no time before it turns heated, sloppy, and erratic. Richard takes him then, on the sand, tearing off those red shorts and kissing every inch of flesh. It's so good. Too good.

He can almost believe it will last.

Chapter 40

They stink.

Smelling strongly of cheap soda, wet towels, and musk. It's late by the time they leave. Richard is ravenous, stomach clenching from all their activities at the lagoon.

Beau suggests they stop by the diner.

He agrees. High, insatiable, touching Beau everywhere he can reach. His favorite part is the space on his lower back, firm and endless, trailing down to his perky ass.

Richard's hand rests there, fingers occasionally dipping beneath his pants, thumbing the fabric of his underwear. He'll often press against Beau's shoulder, standing far too close so that nobody can mistake their intimacy for a friendship.

It's riveting. Casual touches, the strange looks of passer's by trying to gauge their relationship status. Richard is finally out.

And he couldn't give a fuck.

The diner is packed with people. Since Maybelle's arrest, her younger sister Bonnie's been looking after the place. She looks tired, worn thin, but she gives them a welcoming smile. "What can I do for you?"

Richard is drunk on love.

Vision blurring, pink cheeks, and beaming at nothing. Beau is no different, clinging onto him like a spider monkey. They sit beside each other in a booth, their knees plastered together, Beau's arm thrown around his shoulders.

They order something simple. A burger with fries. Richard is too hungry to wait. Beau is wearing a gray t-shirt and those same lovely red shorts. "You shouldn't have worn those shorts."

Beau smirks. "Why not? I reckoned I should wear them before they end up in the trash torn to pieces."

Richard grips his thigh under the table. "You know what those shorts do to me."

"Of course, I know. That's why I wore them."

"Brat."

"You love it," Beau mutters. "I have time off now. I want to enjoy it. Blackwell's always taking life with a grain of salt, a slice of lemon, and a shot of tequila."

Richard laughs. "Is that right? That explains why you keep giving out your money like it's candy."

"Just to people I love," Beau responds, eyes twinkling. "Good thing I'm a pessimist, though I'll never expect the money back."

"You'll never get it back anyway," Richard mutters.

Beau chuckles, leaning into him. "Richard, I don't give a fuck. You being here is enough for me."

His heart lurches.

Heat flames his face as he stares back at Beau in awe. There are so many people around. Richard wishes he could take him into his arms and kiss him silly for saying that.

Why not? a voice whispers to him. Richard swallows, nerves making his hands sweat. *Why not, indeed?* They're out. Together. A large part of him wants to claim him for all the world to see. He's not hiding anymore.

Richard turns to him in the booth, thumbs the beauty mark at the edge of his lips. Beau leans into it, eyes fluttering close.

Those lips are thin, sensual. Richard can't help brushing against them, softly, delicately, like butterfly wings. A simple press. Long enough to inhale his scent, feel the warmth of his skin. It lingers like a buzzing shock. Electrifying.

Beau inhales sharply, smiles, and leans in closer.

Richard must be possessed because he tilts forward, claiming those lips brutishly, beard bristling against virgin flesh. Whatever noises Beau makes are drowned out by feverish kisses.

It's too much. It's not enough.

"Dad?"

They break apart, panting. It's too late. They've been seen. Lana stands there with Roy and the kids, both of them looking perplexed.

Shit.

Richard's been caught. With his tongue down his fairy lover's throat.

~

IT'S AWKWARD.

So very awkward. Lana and Roy look shell-shocked as if this is the last thing they ever expected to see. Richard and Beau detangled, much to their reluctance. Ida stares wide-eyed, and Kyle plops down in the empty seat across from them, eyes beaming. "Do you remember me?"

Beau looks at Richard, then at Roy. "Sure, kid."

"Do you still have your bow?"

"No," Beau replies uneasily. "I had to sell it. Sorry."

"I'm going to buy my own when I get older," Kyle proclaims loudly. Lana and Roy look helpless, watching the events unfold.

Richard jumps into action, forcing a laugh.

"What am I chopped liver? Come, hug me! Is that how you greet your old man?"

Kyle bounces over to him and hugs him, then resumes chatting. Bonnie swoops by their table with two drinks in her hand. "Oh, more people? I'll add more placemats."

"Oh... ah... wait—" Lana calls after her, but she's already gone. "Maybe we should—"

"Might be better if we just head out," Roy says.

"I'm hungry, though!" Kyle whines. "You promised burgers!"

Lana and Roy share a look, then she shrugs and sits down across from Beau in the booth. Roy's jaw works. He guides Ida to a seat before he sits down too. "Family dinner it is."

Bonnie brings placemats and takes all of their orders. The adults sit in tense silence, Kyle happily chatting away about school and other things he's been working on.

Lana keeps most of her attention on Ida, refusing to make eye contact with Richard.

"So, what did you guys do today?" Roy asks, looking between them.

"We went to the beach."

"Sounds good. Nice, especially in this weather."

"Yeah."

God. It's torture. Although Richard desperately wants them all to get along, he has been hoping it wouldn't be in a forced situation.

"I'm sorry."

Beau and Lana are staring at each other, her eyes water as she gazes into his eyes. "We—you don't have to say anything—"

"I didn't know you back then," Beau powers through. "What I did was wrong. I'm sorry. I shouldn't have done that but," he grabs Richard's hand, "I love Richard. I won't hurt him again. I promise."

Lana swallows, and then reaches across the table to hold Beau's hand. "I forgive you. Okay. You did nothing wrong."

Relief washes over Beau's face, and he squeezes her hand tightly. Lana blinks back tears, then offers a small smile. "So, since this is the official meeting. I'd like to get to know you better. What do you do in your spare time?"

The question opens up the flood gates. Beau flourishes, talking about the books he's read, along with the people he's gotten to know over time through his travels. Turns out he's been all across the south, from North Carolina to Virginia and more.

Lana is intrigued, asking questions and sharing her own experiences. It ends with Kyle launching into the story about how Richard got them lost on their way to SixFlags, and they were stranded for ten hours.

"Worst. Vacation. Ever."

Richard swats at Kyle. "You're lucky you even got a vacation, especially with your bad grades."

"Dad!"

"He's right, honey." Lana laughs. "Lord, this kid knows how to work his Bambi eyes, though. One look and I can't say no."

They continue talking, spewing jokes and insults. Richard is breathless, cheeks hurting from smiling too wide. Roy is suspiciously quiet.

With his brows drawn together, a dark expression clouds his face.

CHAPTER 41

THE BIRTHDAY CAKE IS a sordid, dilapidated thing.

Icing melts, dripping precariously around the edges, and it tilts awkwardly to one side. With so many layers, it caves in, crumpling beneath its weight.

Yet, Lana beams with pride.

"Happy birthday, Richard." She kisses his cheek, and Richard laughs.

Roy pats him on the shoulder, squeezing it firmly as he drags him further into the backyard. There are golden party streamers everywhere, a banner that says thirty-four in big block letters.

Beau takes a cone hat from Kyle and is promptly dragged away to see his new collection of toys. People are scattered about, people he hasn't seen or talked to since he went to prison.

Tanya and Hiromi stand around the buffet table, along with Isaac and Lucina. Bonnie appears with Ida next to her, kisses his cheek, and hands him a fruity drink. Houston greets him warmly, along with his very pregnant wife, Karen.

It's strange seeing them all again. They never visited when he was in prison or called when he got out. It seems they were waiting until the dust settled.

"Why did you invite them?" Richard can't help but ask.

Their presence is entirely too confounding.

Roy shrugs. "Lana needed the help, and well... they said they wouldn't mind coming. Look, don't judge them too harshly for not reaching out. The bureau was investigating us after everything... internal affairs had us all by the balls then... Plus, Lucina and Lana are still friends... they respected you so much once... let's just put it all in the past, at least for today."

"Okay."

Just for today. He can do that. The question is: can Beau?

He looks over at him, seeing him indulge with Kyle warms his heart. At some point, Bonnie starts playing with them and Ida, then Isaac and Karen join in.

Richard grabs two plates of food, then looks down at the buffet table. The chicken is burnt to a crisp, the salad looks way too slimy, and beside it, there's something that is supposed to be bread but looks like a solid brick.

The celebration cake is imperfectly perfect. The food looks like it's been prepared blindfolded by Santa's drunkest elf.

And things couldn't be better.

"Eat up! Don't be shy!" Lana nudges his arm.

Richard looks over at Roy helplessly.

I ordered a pizza, Roy mouths at him. Richard nods then fills two plates with food, which he will dump in the garbage.

Later they play pin the tail on the donkey. Richard accidentally ends up pinning it on Roy's face. It's the most fun he's had in years. Even Hiromi keels over with laughter.

The evening wanes, Roy breaks out the hard liquor, and everyone drinks. Beau ends up sandwiched between Isaac and Houston, talking about stocks or something of that nature.

Richard retreats to the kitchen, helping Lana take out the trash. They settle beside each other to do the dishes.

"Thanks for this."

Lana smiles at him. "You're welcome."

"It means a lot."

"I know." She kisses his cheek. "I'm happy for you. Beau is... something special. I know now we were never meant to be... looking back, it always felt like we were good friends. Best friends even, but Roy... he's so passionate... I feel alive around him."

"I know the feeling." Richard bumps her shoulder. "Still. I've never seen him so content. I think he's loved you for a long time."

"I think so too... even in high school... I had my suspicions, but..." She sighs happily. "Anyway... I got a letter in the mail..." Her smile fades. "I want to speak to you about it."

"Okay."

Lana dries her hands, then grabs her purse and retrieves the letter. "Life insurance policy was withdrawn... in the case of terminal illness..." she reads aloud. "Richard, I thought we weren't going to dip into this? Why would they even give you the funds anyway? I don't understand."

Richard swallows thickly.

His hands shake as he tries to gather his response. He's been avoiding this for months. Since Dr. Trevor gave him the news that his life is going to be cut short.

"It's for you and the kids."

"I understand that, but why?" Lana asks. "This is too much. We can't accept it. I got a new job; Roy is doing better than ever before. We don't need it. You already know that. I just don't understand why you would withdraw from it."

"It's for you and the kids for when I'm gone."

Several emotions flash before her face.

Lana stares at him, hands scrunching the paper as she takes a stuttering breath. "What the hell does that mean? Is it your knee? What's going on, Richard?"

He can't breathe.

All the air is sucked out of the room. How can he explain it to her? The words stay lodged in his throat, suffocating him. All he can do is watch as horror explodes all across her face.

"The coma..." he says slowly. "They put me under to control the bleeding in my head... the trauma did irrevocable damage. I... cancer runs in my family... my mom died from it... it's genetic they said... malignant."

"*What* is?" Lana trembles, tears falling from her eyes.

"The tumor."

A plate crashes to the floor.

Richard and Lana start, whirling around to see where the noise came from. Beau stands there quivering, tears streaming down his cheeks as the burnt chicken scatters around the room.

Agony rips across his face.

Utter Betrayal. Beau's face morphs, transforming into a rancorous rage. It shatters Richard, breaking him into a million pieces.

Fuck no.

Beau pivots, torment written all over his face. It wrenches Richard's heart out of his chest as he leaves the kitchen.

CHAPTER 42

RICHARD CHARGES AFTER HIM.

The hallway is short, narrow. It's too hot here. His head is about to burst. Richard grabs onto Beau's shirt, and Beau swings at him violently. "You lying sack of shit!"

Several heads turn.

Richard is too busy to care. The world is crumbling. The sky is falling. Things are disintegrating right before his very eyes. "*Beau*—"

"Don't touch me!"

"Calm down—"

"You liar! You're fucking scum! Just like all the rest!" Beau screams, teeth bared viciously.

"I can explain—"

"There's *nothing* to say! It was a mistake! Everything was a fucking mistake! You bastard! I could kill you for this!"

"Relax," Richard says desperately. Roy, Isaac, and Houston step forward, braced and ready to spring if need be. "I'm not—let me explain—"

"You're leaving. Everyone is leaving. Why does everyone leave?" Beau is sobbing so hard; his tears fall endlessly. "Then go! I don't need you anymore! *Leave!* Fucking leave!" He shoves Richard so hard he stumbles back, kneecap roaring in anguish.

"Richard!" Roy warns.

"Don't—" Richard barks. "Let me handle this. Beau, I am not going anywhere. I can explain. You need to calm down."

Richard lunges, grabbing his arms.

"If I am so worthless, then go!"

Goddamnit. He's had enough.

He moves with a quick start, roughly grabbing Beau's brittle arms and wrenching his entire body forward. He hauls Beau up, encasing him in his arms and lifting him off the ground.

Beau yelps, eyes widening as Richard spins them both around, then barges into the vacant room in the hallway. They slam against the wall, blinding pain shots up his thigh, and his vision whites out.

The common cool callousness fades, burning bright, he alights with deep fire. He wants to shake Beau until his teeth rattle and his legs quake.

Beau turns into a wild animal.

Scratching and gnawing, punching at everything he can reach.

Richard bears all of it.

"Don't touch me!" Beau roars. "Get your hands off me!"

Richard pushes him against the wall, bracketing his arms around Beau's face.

"*Never.*"

That one word enrages Beau.

"I'll never let go. Stop fighting! Listen to me—"

"There's nothing to say! You bastards are all the fucking same! Spouting the same shit! Fuck off and die then! Leave me be!"

"*Beau,*" Richard exclaims. "Look at me—I love you. I love you."

"Do not look at me, Richard," he cries helplessly. "I am worthless."

"Stop it!" Richard grabs his chin roughly. "You're not worthless or any of the fucking shit that's been drilled into your head. I love you, and I'm not going anywhere!"

"But—what you said—you liar—"

"I *am* dying. I will die if I don't get treatment in time."

Beau gazes up at him, eyes splotchy with tears. "You—"

"I have cancer. It's malignant—but they can treat it. At that time, I didn't have money for it. I still don't. The treatments—I can't afford it, and without you, my life has no meaning. So, I withdrew from the account, hoping I could get some money for the treatments and—" He takes a deep breath. "Provide for my family. I didn't mean to deceive you. I just—we *just* got back together. I'm sorry. I was going to tell you. I was going to tell all of you. I didn't have time."

Beau stills beneath him. "You need the funds—"

"I can't ask that of you—"

"I'm giving it," Beau snarls. He grips Richard's arm tightly. "Take it. All of it. I don't care. Just don't leave me. Please don't leave me."

"I'm not. I won't—" Richard wheezes. It's absurd. "I can't."

Beau nods frantically, holding onto him for dear life. He crumples, pressing his forehead against Richard's, panting like mad.

Emotions churn around him. They're both winded, with wild cuts and bruises. It's horrific to have his family witness this. Richard waits for the shame to engulf him, the rabid slew of disgrace, but it doesn't come.

Beau is still with him.

That's all that matters.

"I'm sorry." Beau laughs. It's mirthless. "I've ruined your birthday. I overacted. I just—I can't lose you again."

"You won't," Richard says sternly. "I'm here."

They fall into a tight embrace, Beau quivering from the aftershocks. He cries for so long and so hard that Richard can do nothing but hold him tightly.

All Beau knows is pain, rough, tumultuous waters, tempest, and decay. He knows nothing of kindness, of virility, of steadiness, and unconditional love. His kneecap burns, pain so bad he nearly folds, but he holds strong for Beau.

To be his rock and pillar against the storm.

CHAPTER 43

THEY LEAVE SOON AFTER.

With Beau's face buried in the crook of his neck. Richard retreats, slinking out the back door, ignoring the hasty calls of concerns from his family.

It's too late. He's beaten raw, minced like meat. It feels cowardice to leave this way, yet Beau clings onto him so desperately that Richard can't bear to part with him yet.

It takes fortitude to backtrack.

Eventually, they will find another route for victory, but it's best to go quietly for now. When they arrive home, Beau scurries off to the shower, muttering about grease on his clothes.

Richard watches him silently.

Everything hurts. His arms and face convey a barrage of bruises and scratches, and his knee throbs. Taking some water and paper towel, he dabs slightly, trying to clear off the dried blood.

Beau finds him like that.

Hunched over the kitchen table, trying to stem the flow of blood on his arms and cheek. He wears nothing but a flimsy white towel. It's short, and when he bends, Richard can see the curve of his cock outlined through the fabric.

"Beau—"

"Let me." Beau grabs the antiseptic, dabs it on a cloth, and starts wiping his wounds. The movements are gentle, clean, and precise. He kneels in front of Richard, eyes rimmed with tears, wet hair plastered to his face.

It's servitude.

The actions are revenant, loving, so very graceful that it pierces his heart. His eyes brim with tears, his heart aches in his chest. Beau loves him so much.

He didn't see it before, but he does now.

"I'm sorry I haven't been truthful... I just needed to make sure you would stay."

"I get it now," Beau mutters. "Before... I thought... you were just like the rest... giving me false promises."

"False promises?"

Beau stares at the ground, jaw working. "Of a normal life. A good life. I came back to have a normal life with you. That's all I want. No whoring or drugs. I want to be free. That's why I'm here, to be free with you and when you said... you had cancer... I thought you were just using me... waiting for your life to end so that you could leave me."

"You know I wouldn't ever choose to leave you."

Beau glares at him. "Nobody *chooses* to leave. Yet, they do it all the same. Creed didn't choose to hit a pole, and my daddy didn't choose to have a stroke."

Richard falls silent.

Things are starting to make sense now. In Beau's mind, they left him. Voluntarily or involuntarily, using their pied piper flute, security and happiness went running after their rancid trail. Beau forged his own life.

In the streets, surrounded by wicked men, all he had was his blood and flesh. Jumping from town to town, the world undoubtedly fell into a colorless maze.

Words fell upon deaf ears, light upon shadows. Speaking for years to an audience that had vanished. Not a single soul to turn to.

Loneliness. Richard knew it well.

"I'm sorry. I won't leave you."

It's an empty promise, one he can't possibly keep. If the cancer spreads too far and wide, he'll be dead in a year. All they have is right here and now.

Beau sets his jaw, hands clenching around the cloth. "I'll pay for the surgery. Anything else you need, let me know. I have more than enough. I want to share it. Let me."

There are so many things that can go wrong. What if they trace it back? What if they get caught? But the mulish glint to his eyes cannot be trifled with.

Richard doesn't dare to enrage his fairy lover again.

"I don't want to be alone," Beau says, reaching out to hold his hand.

Richard drags Beau into his arms. "You won't be. I swear it."

Then they're kissing.

Hot and feverish, a stunning battle of tongues and mouths waging war. Richard grunts, lifting Beau and placing him on the kitchen table. He settles between his legs, cupping his cheek and kissing him senselessly.

Beau retaliates, biting down on his lower lip until the coppery taste of blood floods his mouth. Richard pulls away in a gasp, licking at the cut with a frenzied expression on his face.

Richard brings a hand up to grab Beau's jaw tightly and with wild eyes. "Only you make me like this."

Beau makes a show of licking Richard's blood off his lip.

"Good."

Richard drags his face up to kiss him again as if he's helpless to it.

This is what Beau wants. He wants to ruin Richard's meticulously thought-out plans. Drag him so far off course that Richard can't find his way back. Wants to pry the reins from Richard's tight grip and take away the burden for once.

Let Richard breathe.

Richard fumbles for the opening of Beau's towel, desperate and wanton. Beau lifts up and removes the towel, shucks it over his shoulder, and lets Richard run his hands everywhere.

They glide over his thighs that twitch under the attention. Richard thumbs at the bare skin, eyes roaming over the vast amount of skin. His hands touch ridged skin, fissures of old scar tissue from Mason and Gary. Richard kisses each scar he can reach, a soft press of lips. Then pulls away.

Beau's stare is molten.

Richard feels he could melt from under it.

"Don't be gentle. Not tonight."

Richard's grip tightens. Dipping back, he kisses Beau again, hands fumbling to undo his belt buckle. Beau bites down on his lower lip, moaning softly.

Richard exhales. "Lube?"

"No need."

Beau grabs his wrists then he brings one of Richard's hands up to his entrance, which is already sodden and stretched with lube. Beau grabs a condom out of Richard's back pocket and makes a show of ripping it open and rolling it on his aching cock.

How the condom got there is another story entirely.

CHAPTER 44

RICHARD MAKES A DISTRESSED noise deep in the back of his throat and whispers his name again. Reverent. Once properly slick, Beau pulls off.

"Do it. Fuck me."

With a groan, Richard knocks their foreheads together again. "If you keep speaking like this, I'm not going to last very long."

With a chuckle, Beau slides his hands down to guide Richard's cock to his entrance. "Come now. Fuck me already."

With renewed vigor, Richard slides down to bite at the soft skin of Beau's neck, pressing down harder and harder with his teeth until Beau groans and there's a flower of dark purple beneath the skin. His hips push forward again until the wet cockhead is pressing against Beau's entrance.

Richard pushes his cock in. It's so tight. Marvelous. A bitten-off moan rips through his throat. He thrusts, quick and deep, buried to the hilt. "Your mine," he says, pulling out again, the tip resting snugly inside Beau's rim, and then fucks into him with such force, Beau cries out.

"Ahhh," Beau groans out, and Richard snaps his hips harder and harder, feeling an inferno blaze within.

"*Fuck*," Richard pants.

Beau grits his teeth and grabs at the fabric of Richard's sleeves, biting out an embarrassingly breathy, "Shut up."

Richard hums, pleased, and then slides one hand up to wrap around Beau's neck with such a look of barely contained hunger that Beau leans his head back further to give Richard better access.

Fuck. It's way too much. Emotions take over, and he can barely stand it. Through the blur of tears, he moans out Beau's name, squeezing his neck so tightly.

Beau chokes, throat rattling for air as he wheezes desperately.

He continues fucking into Beau like that. Unforgiving, cruel, and heartbroken, and when he comes, he comes buried deep inside of Beau, blocking off any air that Beau can gasp for until he briefly loses consciousness. *Don't leave me.*

I can't. Richard wants to cry back. It's all over. He releases Beau's neck, noticing the purplish marks on his throat. Haunting. Beautiful.

Beau looks like he's been fucked by a wild animal. It must hurt. To love so fiercely.

Tears streak his cheeks. Richard takes Beau's cock in his hands, falling slowly to his knees to take it into his mouth in one fell swoop.

Beau hisses, back arching off the table as he groans. It doesn't take long. Maybe a few minutes or less. He sucks Beau's cock into his mouth, plunging his fingers in his tight hole, hitting that spot over and over again until Beau sobs from pleasure.

Spend floods his mouth, hot and potent. Richard drinks it all like sweet nectar. When it's over, Beau curls into a ball, shaking, sweating. Face matted with tears and bodily fluids.

Exhaustion finally takes over. "Beau."

"I can't feel my legs." Beau lets out a wet laugh, still trembling from the aftershocks. Richard gets off the ground, takes Beau into his arms, and carries him to the bedroom.

They fall on the bed ingeniously. The throbbing in his knee turns into hellfire. Richard takes his medication, then pulls Beau into his arms.

"Richard. *Richard*." Beau's voice is raspy, breathy against his collarbone. "I feel you. I still feel you inside me. In my soul."

Good, that's the only place I long to be.

~

IN THE DISTANCE, he hears them.

Outside his window, piston fires. Blender's full of bolts. Motorcycles race down the paved roads, their engines deafening at this early hour. There's a sea of black jackets, men with helmets and thunderous expressions.

Bandidos. The writing is crisp, blood-red, and yellow, unlike the Rebel Brotherhood. Richard watches as they tear through the streets of Byrmonville, tires squealing.

A war is brewing.

That explains Roy's attitude. It must be big. Richard cracks open his living room window. The humidity still manages to make it all very stifling. He has just started his breakfast, when the phone rings.

"Everything okay?" Roy's voice booms on the other end.

Richard hums, tipping the frying pan to remove the excess grease. "We're fine. Sorry... about yesterday..."

"It's okay—but fuck, man," Roy sighs. "We were worried. We thought he was going to kill you."

"I'm sure he was." Richard chuckles, dumping some cream into his coffee. "It's okay. Things are... different now."

"Still, man," Roy continues. "It's fucked up. Lana is still pissed that you didn't tell her about the cancer. She's mad at me for keeping it a secret too."

"I'll explain," Richard promises. "Give me some time, but the kids won't have to worry about anything. I can take care of it."

"That's not the point," Roy mutters. "You can't just—we depend on you too, Richard. You need to take better care of yourself. We can work out payment plans, medical bills can be split up—just get better—"

"I'll be fine," Richard interrupts. "Don't worry. I've got it covered."

"If you say so."

Richard bristles. "Anything else?"

There's a pause, long enough to think maybe he hung up.

"Not at all."

Then the line goes dead.

CHAPTER 45

PULSING BASS THRUMS IN the air.

It's hot, sticky. He can barely breathe in the cramped space at the bar. The music is so loud it makes him dizzy, clouds of smoke in the air. Beau is somewhere near the back finishing up, counting receipts and whatnot.

Richard hates parties.

However, Beau texted him, apologetic and wanton. Asking for forgiveness for being late to dinner for the third time this week. It's fine.

It's not.

Richard hates the absence, the pang in his chest whenever Beau cancels again. Yet, he always makes it home before midnight. Crawls into bed, plastering himself to Richard's side, and kisses him silly.

Richard thought he explained that. Alas, he doesn't want to cling too hard, hold too tightly. For his fairy lover may break, cracking under the immense pressure of his love.

So, he sits at the bar, nursing water, watching the throes of people strutting around. Most of the men wear the Rebel Brotherhood jackets, their smiles are wide, lazy.

"As I live and breathe." Neil slithers beside him, smelling strongly of booze and something else.

Something toxic.

"You again." Neil smiles, too wide to be natural. "Beau must have you on a pretty tight leash."

"And vice versa," Richard mutters, sipping his drink.

Neil laughs. "You know... Beau hasn't been this relaxed in a long time... I reckon you had something to do with that."

It's all an act. To rile him up. Richard realizes now that Neil likes to push buttons until he gets the reaction that he wants. Well, he's going to be sorely mistaken. Richard isn't going to give him the time of day.

Beau comes out from behind the curtains; his eyes are somewhat glassy as he strides over to them. Due to his palpable charisma, at one glance, Richard's heart jolts.

"Hey." He crowds Richard's space. His stomach backflips, noting all the men around them staring. Was Beau usually like this? "Thanks for coming. I'll be done soon. Give me ten minutes or so."

"Take your time."

His dark eyes never leave Richard's face. "You're pissed. I can see it in your eyes. I'll finish up right now."

Is it that obvious? Richard softens.

"I'm fucking up a lot lately. I know. Just give me a minute. I'll be out soon." Before Richard can respond, Beau kisses him gently on the lips. "Don't leave."

Heat engulfs him. It spreads down his cheeks and neck. Neil tips his drink at him in a mock salute, then turns toward the person beside him to carry on a conversation.

Is Beau out? It seems so. None of these men so much as batted an eye when they kissed. How strange. Richard's lips tingle, he grins tenderly as he takes another sip of his water. Several moments pass before Beau walks out; the music fades as he struts toward him.

This time Richard welcomes it.

Chuckling low and deep, before lips seal over his, frantic and bruising. Beau is drunk. Richard can taste the beer on his tongue. It's marvelous.

The place is devoid of gravity.

Richard floats, light as ash, higher above the rest.

"I want you so badly," Beau mutters against his lips. "I don't think I can wait."

Richard grabs his waist, pressing their bodies together against the bar. "Don't tease me."

"Why not?" Beau puffs a laugh, kissing him again. "I love to tease you."

A thrill shoots through him.

"Let's get out of here." Beau nuzzles against him. "I'll suck you off in the parking lot—"

Richard puffs a laugh, but it cuts off as Beau runs his hand up to his thigh. *Christ*—there are people around. He nibbles on Beau's ear, kissing a desperate trail down his cheek and neck.

The door slams open.

The music cuts and Richard sits knee-deep in silence. The faucet drips into the bar sink, each drop reverberating around the room like a cymbal.

Nobody blinks.

Beau pulls away, eyes meeting Neil's as nine strangers walk in.

Slicked back hair, goatees, and sharp eyes, the leader strides in confidently. His body is muscular, relaxed. Leather stretches across his forearms and chest.

Bandidos.

In their territory. The fragile peace is over before it even has the chance to take root. Dread engulfs Richard's core. They've come, at long last, to take back what's been stolen from them.

By nightfall, there will be nothing left, just a whisper of a kiss, the shadow of warmth from a lover's embrace. It could mean Beau's untimely death.

The hairs raise at the back of his neck as the men around them rally. The air is so brittle it could snap, and if it doesn't, he might. They're brazen. Suicidal. To come here unannounced, into the lion's den.

Neil gets up from his seat at the bar. He smiles, slow and deliberate. Two gangs, both with the intent to maim and kill. Beau slips away from him, and Richard watches with widening eyes as he steps toward Neil.

They share a look.

Not like before. This one is very different. A silent conversation, to which Neil bends his head, an offer of submission. *What the fuck is going on?* The bodyguard from before flanks them, then another, and then another.

Beau levels them all, a signal. No words are spoken. They move as one. A carefully constructed organism, taking its lead from the head.

The ground falls away from his feet. Richard stares at them in horror. Who exactly is the leader of the Rebel Brotherhood? Neil steps *behind* Beau, hands poised, ready to fight.

Richard's stomach turns.

Chapter 46

THE WINDS DASH INTO his face, causing the skin to tug in the opposite direction. His stomach roils, scorching and copious bile threatens to erupt.

Who is Beau Blackwell?

Is he the victim of Byrmonville? The worthless prostitute that needed to be saved by the sheriff or is he the cunning human trafficker? Pushing drugs and other means to ensure his survival?

Christ—he doesn't know. Will he ever?

He's the leader, Enos said once, which Richard completely disregarded. All the evidence is there, right before his eyes, yet he always chose to ignore it.

Richard falls straight to his death. Gut-wrenching, heart pounding loudly in his chest. The pain is immeasurable yet welcomed amidst the chaos. He wants to reach out, hold on to something, anything to quell the panic.

They lock eyes, and Richard finally understands.

It's not about what was, it's about what is. Beau belongs to him. They're one. Richard has always known being a cop wouldn't last long.

"Demonio Blanco," the man spits, glaring viciously at Beau. "*—danos el dinero que te llevaste!*"

Beau smirks.

"*Mataste a nuestro líder, lo cortaste en pedazos. Nosotros queremos justicia!*" the man continues, stepping forward menacingly.

"*No encontrarás ninguno aquí,*" Beau replies, fluent and steady.

"*Ustedes bastardos. ¡Debería matarte!*"

"*Intentalo,*"

The man reels back, eyes widening in disbelief.

"*Yo soy el diablo blanco.*"

The man rips out his gun.

Beau lunges forward, grabbing his wrist, wrenching the gun from his hand. Beau moves fast, like a blur, as he punches the man in the face.

He reels back, blood spurts from his nose. Beau's fists move in quick succession, landing several crippling blows to his stomach and kidney.

The Bandidos swarm, whipping out their guns, firing shots into the air. Richard ducks, heart in his throat as he crawls under the bar and holes up behind it.

Fuck—Beau. He can't move. The bullets tear through the wooden bar stools, shredding them to pieces. He manages to look through a small hole, spotting Beau in the midst of it all.

Everything sails past him.

Beau is possessed, taking on several guys at once, beating them all into a bloody pulp. The leader staggers forward, yanked back with Beau's right forearm. Time slows down, and the world dissipates as Richard watches on in horror.

Beau grabs his neck, snapping it like a tree branch. The Bandidos shrill, guns firing rapidly without purchase, and Neil leaped straight into the fray, swinging a baseball bat.

It's pure carnage.

Richard is shocked. Horrified, disgusted. Yet, oddly intrigued. The demon is restless, blistering beside him, ready to spring into action.

A man springs up behind Beau, and Richard moves swiftly.

He tackles the Bandido, drilling into him like a linebacker from his blindside. It's a clean hit. Shoulder to shoulder that arches his spine. Fuck, it hurts. Richard feels the judder as they clatter to the ground.

The man twists around, swerving with a wayward snake and punching him in the face. Richard expects it, anticipates it, and then bangs his nose against his forehead, knocking him out cold.

It's a blood bath.

Several Bandidos take the fallen man's place, swarming him in a sea of fists and kicks. Richard claws his way to the top, moving with deadly precision until his knuckles bleed.

Fuck, what a rush. He hits and kicks, driving each man back and retreating out the door they came. The Rebel Brotherhood men howl in triumph. The place is trashed, several men lay on the ground, not moving.

Beau throws his arms around his shoulders, hysterically pawing at him. "Are you hurt? Are you okay?"

"I'm fine," Richard shouts over the raucous noise.

Beau kisses him brutally.

Neil slinks out the back door, his large form retreating as the other men grab their guns and anything else they can carry. Richard grips Beau's waist. It's madness. Pure and simple. The Bandidos have them ambushed. Any attempt at an escape could mark their brutal end.

Richard thinks back to the conversation the leader had with Beau.

From his years on the force, he's picked up Spanish here and there. Mostly to assist with helping families that needed a translation.

Beau's mother had been from Guatemala and was found dead in a buoy outside the Blackwell property not long after moving to Byrmonville.

Yo soy el diablo blanco.

I am the white devil.

Chapter 47

Fear grips him, threatening to take over. It sits like an angry ball, propelling toward him with each breathe. The air is stale, and the weather is stifling.

Each man grabs a weapon from the back, locked and loaded, awaiting their next orders. Beau transforms before his eyes. Gone is the nimble body ducking and squawking. Before him now stands a man built on ruthlessness and revenge.

"How many?" Beau barks.

"Fifteen AK-47's pointed at the back and front." Tanner steps forward.

"Escape routes?"

"Fire escape." Tanner shakes his head. "No way out."

"Then we must go through," Beau mutters. He detangles from Richard, reaching deep into a duffle bag to pull out two detonations. "Strike now."

Tanner nods and then passes them to two other guys.

Richard's anxiety claws at his throat. Where the fuck did Beau get hand detonations from? Is there a bomb nearby? Everything is happening way too fast. It's triggering his PTSD. He's suspended in horror that this will all end so very wrong.

"Trust me." Beau grabs his arm, steering him to the back.

They duck very low behind a pillar both ready to scramble behind the bar. Tanner and several other guys stay low toward the windows. Everyone else is in a state of frantic frenzy, hiding under tables and chairs.

Half of them won't make it.

There'll be collateral. Just like the war.

His eyes swing to Beau's, manic and afraid, and yet it evaporates instantly. Beau holds his hand, grip sturdy as he nods to Tanner. *Trust me.*

This time, he does.

Before he can inhale, his body is struck by a giant force. It rocks him so powerfully, he falls back.

Richard recoils.

Blinded by searing agony as it tears him apart. Another impact tosses them into the air. He rolls, all of him aches, head pounding mercilessly.

Pain judders through him, blood soaks his shirt and pants, as holes ripe through what's left of the bar.

Something is cooking, burning.

Sulfur and ash. Fire rages from the stage as the speakers catch alight. People run. They fly from the bar and straight through the open door.

Richard can't breathe. His tongue is heavy, and he cannot swallow or do anything. An animal scream erupts from his throat as he chokes on blood and bile.

Beau is there, hauling him forward with immense strength.

There is a cut on his lower brow, a wound spanning the length of his arm, but his eyes are clear and lethal. They stumble through the door. The carnage before them is enough to make the strongest man hurl.

Dead bodies.

Hundreds of them, most in leather jackets of the Bandidos. Their bikes are decimated, bits and pieces scattered everywhere.

Richard is caught in agony. It's incomprehensible.

Beau drags him away toward the end of the road. Richard pukes, stomach-wrenching hard as he bends over.

Beau stands beside him, drenched in blood and sweat. His shirt clings to his muscular form as he gazes at the skyline.

The wail of sirens sounds in the distance, and Richard doesn't move from his spot. Beau runs his hands through his hair gently, soothingly.

Emergency sirens call out into the river of traffic, and where once there was no way forward, a wide swath opens for the blue to flow right through.

~

"HOW THE fuck did this happen?"

Roy is feral, pacing back and forth as the officers and EMT run around behind them. Richard sits at the back of the EMT ambulance, knee wrapped in gauze as they examine him for the fifth time. Beau's arm is swathed, with a few cuts and bruises on his head, but he is otherwise unscathed.

Most of the men in the Rebel Brotherhood walked away unharmed.

Beau takes out a cigarette, lights it, takes a slow drag, then shrugs. "Dunno."

Roy looks murderous.

Richard almost starts laughing. How can he explain this?

The most important thing is that there is more to Beau than meets the eye. "We were attacked by the Bandidos," Richard explains. "They appeared with guns. It was self-defense."

"Self-defense?" Roy spits. "Half of them were blown to pieces! In what universe does that make any fucking sense?"

Isaac approaches them, carrying a wad of chard debris and pipes with him. He leans over to whisper in Roy's ear, and his expression changes slightly. "I see," Roy says. "Thanks."

Isaac walks away, taking the evidence with him.

"Turns out the explosion happened in the building behind them. They haven't determined the cause of it yet. Speculation is that it was caused by ammonium nitrate. Kept in the building for farming." Roy side eyes them. "How convenient."

"Looks like it," Beau mutters, taking another drag.

"Why is it every fucking time you're around, there's trouble? It hasn't even been six months, and already Richard is dragged through all kinds of shit—"

"Roy, enough—" Richard steps between them.

"No, it's not enough," Roy seethes. "Can't you see what's happening? He's twisting you around again, turning you into something you're not. He can't come back and fuck up your life like this again."

"I fucked up my life," Richard snaps. "Beau didn't do anything. Okay? Let's be clear about that. I know you think you're looking out for me, but I'm fine. He is the one I love. I choose him, and that's all there is to it."

Roy shakes his head.

"I'm fine," Richard promises.

"Boss!" Houston jogs over to him. "We've got a big fucking problem!"

"What is it?" Roy snarls. "I'm in the middle of something—"

"The precinct is on fire!" Houston exclaims. "That's not even the worst of it. Maybelle and Damian have gone missing."

"Oh fuck!" Roy takes off with Houston hot on his heels.

"Jesus," Richard murmurers. "What the fuck is happening?"

"Dunno," Beau replies. "Stay here, I need to talk to the guys, and then I'll be back."

Richards nods and watches him leave. The area is eerily quiet. There are so many EMTs around, rushing away dead bodies and examining those that have been hurt in the crash.

Richard stands on shaky legs, walking to the edge of the sidewalk away from all the commotion. It must be well after midnight. He's beyond exhausted.

Upon hearing light footsteps, he turns and smiles.

"Back already?"

"Not quite."

Everything fades to black.

CHAPTER 48

RICHARD AWAKES TO THE sound of breaking glass.

His wounds throb. He feels as if his bones are liquid; shards of pain shrink and expand as if they are ripples over the water. Richard groans, touching his head as he struggles to sit up.

What the fuck happened? He touches the soil. It's rich and dewy, staining his hands and fingernails. There's a commotion to his right. He strains his neck as he hears muffled cries.

"Shut up!" someone hisses.

A woman cries out, sniffling. "You don't have to do this."

"Yes, I do!"

The sound of a smack rings out in the room, and Richard slowly creeps back. He doesn't know where he is or who is around him. It's pitch black; the only thing he can make out is the outline of wood. He feels around, noting the smell of old hay and the braying of farm animals.

Richard's fingers brush against iron bolts, trailing up a ladder rising to a loft. He looks up and sees the large storages of hay and stray.

Monroe's farm.

What the hell is he doing here? Richard checks his pockets, he doesn't have anything in terms of a weapon, but that doesn't mean he can't fight back.

"You're a filthy slut, do you know that?" a man snarls. "Teasing me every second of every fucking day! Goddamn whore! You deserved it."

"Damian, please."

Oh, fuck—that means it must be Maybelle he's got there. Richard keeps low, grabbing a rusty pitchfork. He crouches behind a large haystack, looking over to see Damian pinning Maybelle to the ground, her shirt's been torn off, exposing her bra, and it seems he's working on getting her pants off.

Richard's stomach roils, anger burns bright and heavy in his core. *The sick bastard*.

"Get the fuck off her," Richard growls, charging forward and swinging the pitchfork, violently knocking Damian in the head.

The force of the blow makes his head reel back, blood spurts from his nose and mouth as he's flies backward onto the ground. Maybelle scrambles to get away, her hands are bound tight with duct tape, and there's a black bag over her face.

"Stay behind me," Richard barks, guiding Maybelle to her feet.

Damian sputters with laughter, his entire body shakes, and he moves to get on his feet. Under the moonlight, Richard can now see his vital mistake. Damian steps toward them, the gun heavy in his hand.

"Give her back."

Richard steels his nerves, mind racing on what to do next. Damian could shoot him point-blank; the way they were positioned, made it clear he had the upper hand.

"Leave her alone."

Damian doesn't respond. His eyes are black, large sucking voids. Shaky hands, the sheen of sweat covering his lip and brow, pupils were blown wide.

He's high.

That's even worse. That means he won't be thinking properly. Any shots fired might end up killing them both.

"What do you want?" Richard keeps his voice steady, taking a step back and hoping Maybelle will follow his lead.

"Justice," Damian spits. "I want fucking justice from everything this town has done to me!"

Richard stares back at him, puzzled.

Justice? What the hell does that mean? What did Byrmonville do to him? From what he knows of Damian, he is Casey's eldest son.

Is that why he killed her? To rid himself of the guilt and shame?

"Whatever happened… it's not your fault…" Richard raises his hands in surrender. "I'm on your side. Put the gun down, and we can talk about it."

"There's nothing to say!" Damian spits. "Those girls were sluts! All of them deserved what they got! Mother even said so! I would—I would never hurt her! She was everything to me!" His eyes fill with tears as he takes deep, stuttering breaths. "How can they say that—pin that shit on me? I thought we were all brothers! That's what they said—that it was a brotherhood—"

Rebel Brotherhood.

That explains why Richard saw him hanging around, talking shit with the men and asking Neil for a hit. They didn't seem to particularly like him. Then again, why didn't Beau say anything?

Nothing makes sense.

"Damian," Richard says coolly. "Why are am I here?"

"Why shouldn't you be here?" Damian explodes. "You're the most important person to him, of course, you'd fucking be here. He ruined my life! Set me up for crimes I didn't commit, Of course I'd gut the bastard."

Roy's words ring loudly in his ears. *Turns out Damian does some part-time work downtown at a paint shop. They noticed some of their materials missing, all we need to do is match the handwriting, and with his full confession, we can have him convicted.*

"You're all guilty" had been written on the precinct wall. The question that remains is "who" is guilty. *Casey was his mother and his only ally. Without her, the rape charges against him would probably have him thrown away in a federal prison.*

I think it's bigger than Casey and everything else going on. Remember what Monroe said? About some new guy buying up all the property in Brymonville.

CHAPTER 49

Is it possible Damian is being set up?

Forced to take the fall for crimes he didn't commit? What about his molestation against Maybelle? That had been proven true.

That means someone else behind the scenes is working against them to frame Damian for Casey's murder.

It seems she was there. The cameras picked her up near the back. If you look through them, she's pacing back and forth almost as if she's waiting for someone.

That night Maybelle had visited him. *I'm so stressed, between the diner and the grocery store, I never get a moment to myself—I can't—I didn't mean to—I just needed it all to go away!*

Drugs. They were both addicts waiting for their next hit. This means someone arranged for them to be at the bar at a certain time, and that same person knew that they would both be captured on camera hours before Casey's death.

"Who did?"

Damian stomps forward. "Who the fuck do you think—"

Richard sees his shadow, a whisper of movement, and dives to the ground.

A spray of bullets tears through the line of front windows, striking a side wall, shattering a beautiful gilded mirror. It pierces Damian's chest, his body jerks several times, and blood blasts from his body as he falls to the ground.

A lone figure walks toward them, gun held high as they make their way through the barn.

"Richard?"

He breathes a sigh of relief and helps Maybelle stand up. "Here!"

The man runs over, hauling Richard into a tight embrace. "Scared me half to death."

"I'm alright, Beau." Richard cradles his face, kissing him lightly. "Help me get her out of this."

They cut the tap off her arms and remove the bag. Maybelle's face is tear-streaked, and her wrists are heavily bruised. Beau reaches into his back pocket to call the police then helps Richard walk out of the barn, keeping his arm clasped around his waist.

It's been a crazy night. Richard can barely wrap his head around it. "How did you find us?"

Beau's eyes flicker to the tree line. "This is Monroe's property. It's the closest one to the bar. I figured that's where he took you guys."

"How did you know it was Damian?" Richard can't help but ask.

"A hunch is all."

One question burns on his tongue. It's scorching and insistent.

Where did Beau get the gun?

~

IT'S A SHIT show.

Roy brings them all down to the station to get their statements. The back of the station is burnt beyond recognition.

Tanya writes it all down, but he can tell that the case is already closed. They suspected Damian of arson since they caught him on video escaping and setting the police station on fire.

"I don't understand," Richard says to Tanya. "He was in the cell... how did he escape? How did he get the resources to start a fire?"

"We're still investigating it, most likely someone forgot to lock his cell, or he was able to pick it. The bars are pretty old. I am hoping forensics can get back to us in time."

"And the murder weapon? Was Damian guilty of killing Casey?"

"Oh yeah, we found the weapon in his house under the kitchen sink. It seems he wanted her dead for a long time."

I would—I would never hurt her! She was everything to me!

Richard nods but doesn't comment. "Maybelle okay to go home?"

"Yup, Monroe has her on track for rehabilitation. Hopefully, that should get her on the right track going forward."

"Do you know how she got hooked? Did anyone approach her about it?"

"I'll ask around," Tanya says, then offers him a small smile. "Thanks for saving her. I'm sure Monroe appreciates it."

"I didn't save her," Richard mutters.

"Really? On the report, Beau says that you shot Damian and helped them leave the barn."

What?

Why would Beau do that?

Richard keeps his face neutral, but his insides are screaming. "Thanks. I'll be on my way now."

"Of course." She lets him go, and he takes his time walking out of the station.

Stepping out into the night air felt different. Richard takes in the twilight, the rising of mulberry against the backdrop of mauve. Fire-fighters and EMTs hover around the station, their brightly colored uniforms luminous in the rising light.

Between the crowds comes a sudden rising of energy, a joy thrumming for a long-awaited victory. Over what or whom, Richard isn't entirely sure.

It seems the men and women of Byrmonville all banded together to put out the fire at the station. Various people in different stages of undress were aiding officers and civilians alike.

Even the Rebel Brotherhood, in their sleek leather jackets, help carry out wooden planks, blackened by fire.

Amidst the crowd, he feels as if he is a raindrop, protesting to join the ocean. Richard longs for solitude, the ache in his legs and arms grows exponentially, and when he thinks he can't take another step, sturdy arms engulf him.

Beau looks regal against the rising sun, smile small and secret. Home. It crinkles in his eyes, shining light so raw and true that Richard feels it in every cell of his body.

Under the lantern-shine of the sun's golden rays mingled with the first light of a new day, Richard lets his love guide the way.

Chapter 50

Sunset blossoms upon the cloud as sweet wild lavender. A rosy tropical hue cascades around them, the afterglow of the day-long gone, retreating into night.

Beau is beautiful like this, halfway ruined and so utterly at Richard's mercy.

His mouth pressed against the tight abs on Beau's trembling stomach. He licks, making his way down with his lips and teeth. Beau whines low in his throat, and it transforms into a deep moan as Richard's mouth wraps around his cock.

His tongue flicks over the slit, savoring the taste.

Beau shivers, tugging at his hair. "Don't tease, please. It feels so good."

Richard smirks, sucking harder and simultaneously shoving four fingers into him. Beau keens, throwing his head back, knees falling open, a gesture of wild submission.

A thrill shoots down his spine; satisfaction curls in his gut. *After years of wanting and waiting, it's all mine.* Beau's hole flutters around his fingers, flexing as they pump in and out.

Richard marvels in the hot pressure around his knuckles, the way Beau yields so effortlessly to his touch.

The maddening sounds pour from his lips each time Richard bobs his head, torturously engulfing his cock from tip to root. By the time it hits the back of his throat, Beau is a mess, shaking and quivering, tears staining his lovely cheeks to hold himself still.

His hole is gaping, wide and inviting, slick with lube.

"Richard," Beau whispers wetly. Richard absorbs the sound, soaking it up like a sponge. It settles into the shape of something nameless that makes his chest tight.

His wounds from earlier stand stark against his usually unblemished skin. It's glorious. The demon ruffles around him, large talons dig like hooks into meaty flesh.

"Richard," his voice cracks, harsh and pleading, on the brink.

It makes him delirious. His free hands run up Beau's inner thigh, rubbing his thumb in soothing circles. Then he hooks those long pale knees over his shoulders, taking his cock down.

Beau chokes, whatever words he wanted to say splinter into a sob.

Beau's hands tighten violently in Richard's hair.

Disregarding the pain prickling all along his scalp, Richard drives his fingers deep into Beau and simultaneously presses his thumb into the soft skin behind his balls.

Beau cries out, thrashing under Richard's skillful hands and fingers, hips desperately thrusting. Adrenaline roars in his ears. Richard holds him down, fucking into him ruthlessly while his throat works around his cock.

Beau erupts in his mouth, screams broken off into a deep wail.

Richard seals his lips, swallows, and then swallows again. It seems to last ages, to which Richard's jaw works drinking and drinking his sweet nectar. When it's over, he presses kisses to his stomach and thighs; his skin smells of sex and sweat, and something singularly Beau.

"Richard—I can't take anymore—please—"

Richard jerks his fingers, moving them with quick purpose.

"I know you can."

Beau moans again, stretching out those endless legs, hooking his own hands behind his knees.

A rush of something too sweet to be lust floods through him at the sight of Beau's tear-streaked face. Richard can't wait for a second longer. He's already too far at the edge.

He fists his cock, staring down at the lovely creature before him.

Beau blinks up at him through his tears. "Richard—aren't you—"

"Not tonight," Richard says gruffly. "Hold still. Stay open for me."

Richard strokes himself hard and fast, taking in the pink tint to his fairy lover's chest, the rise and fall of his pulsating hole as it twitches and spills with sleekness.

Biting his lip, Beau stares up at him, emerald eyes twinkling with stardust. As if he'd rather be nowhere else, as if he'd wait an eternity.

Richard grunts, coming on his pale thighs and fucked out hole.

~

"DOES IT HURT?" Beau asks, trailing his fingers down the gash on his arm and knee.

Like a bitch, Richard wants to say but refrains. "Losing you hurts more."

"You never told me... what happened in prison."

Richard gives him a sad smile. "I've never told anyone."

"Why?"

Before seems to exist in the context of his mind, somewhere deep and unfathomable where he can't reach. Prison was a long time ago. He recalls the rancid stench of vile men, the constant beatings, the animalistic nature that seem to wade within.

He doesn't remember who attacked him or why. All he knows is that he spent six months of his time in a coma. After he was released, he spent his second half in rehabilitation for his busted kneecap.

That broke him. The inability to do simple things, like move around normally. He was still in prison, but a different kind.

"Because it doesn't matter."

Beau goes quiet, and his fingers threading through small hairs on his chest. "You matter."

Those words, once spoken to a rough, distrusting teen, with a foul mouth and equally bad attitude. Richard chuckles lowly, then kisses him. "I don't know who attacked me or why. All I know is that they must have hated me, mostly because they didn't kill me. They wanted me alive but incapacitated."

"Bastards," Beau spits, shaking his head. "Fucking bastards."

Richard doesn't comment. If he does, he knows it'll open doors that need to stay firmly closed. "As I said, it doesn't matter. I have you now. That's all I want."

"What if..." Beau says cautiously. "I'm not the person you think I am? What if things are different?"

"I don't care." He never did. "I just want you, in any capacity I can have you. That's all I want."

"Then you'll agree to get chemo and the surgery for your knee?"

Richard shifts in the bed uncomfortably. Of course, he'll do it. For Beau, for his family. Yet, he's afraid of what the outcome may bring. What if they can't cure him? What if he's worse off than ever before. "I'll do it, you know I will, but I—what if—"

"I'm here for good, Richard," Beau says strongly. "I'm not leaving ever again."

CHAPTER 51

SIX MONTHS LATER...

RICHARD HADN'T PLANNED ON telling him, but he knew Beau would figure it out one way or another. His first instinct, after the diagnosis with cancer, had been to hide it.

Only the demon would fret, the monster being trapped inside a gilded cage, ready to take his soul to the devil when the time came.

He welcomed it: death.

For so long, Richard rationalized that he deserved it. Men like him, bloodsucking demons that prey on the lives of others. And yet, Beau shattered all of that.

Wormed his way into his life, giving him reason and will to move on from the past and stride toward the future.

It isn't pretty.

The knee surgery incapacitates him for months, making Beau his only reliable source. They bicker, clawing at each other's throats at little things until they become insurmountable.

~

RICHARD PREPARED for this.

At least he's tried too mentally. However, he knows that perhaps he has been naïve in thinking Beau has done the same.

It's not a good day. He can tell the minute Dr. Trevor opens the door to his room and tells him it's going to be bad.

It's worse.

Richard comes back after a long day. His hospital robes hanging off his arm. He's sluggish, barely shuffling his feet with the aid of three nurses.

Beau leaps from his chair, watching with tear-streaked cheeks as Richard leans heavily against the door. Richard is too skinny, with more bones than flesh.

He can barely hold himself upright.

The nurses steady him, then leave. Shadows of exhaustion and pain lie all over his face. Beau doesn't say a word; he steps forward, puts his arms around him, and says "Richard, let's go." He gives in.

Richard can tell Beau wants to look away, jaw working as he guides Richard toward the bed.

"I'm sorry," Richard chokes. "I didn't want you to see me like this."

"What can I do for you?" Beau asks, crouching down in front of him. "I'll do anything."

"Just be here," Richard replies with a sigh. "Be here and..." don't let me die alone.

"Anything," Beau promises and climbs into the bed beside him.

Beau doesn't sleep, his eyes are wide and bloodshot come the next morning. Richard wants to tell him to go home, that being here will do nothing to speed up his recovery, but he knows it will all fall on deaf ears.

This is their new life now.

~

BEAU NEVER LEAVES.

He stays as if he were a tree rooted to the ground.

Richard comes to rely on his steadiness. The chemo is a different story entirely. Since his stage is advanced, they must be aggressive, which means the treatment is harsh and unrelenting.

It withers his body. He loses weight, his hair falls out, skin turns weak and brittle. Kyle cries when he sees Richard in the hospital, clutching his waist and begging him not to leave.

Lana visits almost daily, with Ida and Roy in tow.

They keep him company, and to show solidarity, Beau and Kyle both shave their heads too. Richard laughs so hard he cries, depressed and lonely in the hospital bed.

When they aren't able to make love anymore, and Richard can only remain flaccid due to the pain, Beau just holds him close, whispering his love and devotion over and over again.

"I've waited an eternity for you."

Richard knows it's true.

Who could ever love a whore? Richard does, immensely, unequivocally. When it's over, it's truly over. Richard is released from the hospital after four months. The doctors and nurses applaud as he takes his first steps toward the bell and rings it loud and clear.

Cancer remission.

Beau kisses him hard as tears of bitter elation fall from his eyes. They're free, finally, finally free.

EPILOGUE

FAMILY AND FRIENDS GATHER together at Greene's Diner.

It's a happy affair. Most of them bring gifts and well wishes, patting Richard on the back and shaking his hand. Roy glides up to him, a suave smile on his lips, nursing a drink.

A homemade banner is situated at the front, with lovely decorative rainbow balloons. Kyle's sloppy handwriting makes it look very charming, along with Ida's writing attempts.

"The rainbow color theme was my idea," Roy says, nudging his arm.

"Thanks," Richard says dryly. "I don't think it could get any gayer in here."

Roy holds up rainbow hats and party horns.

"Never mind."

Roy laughs, patting him on the shoulder. "You deserve it, brother."

"Thank you... for everything..." They haven't always seen eye to eye, but Roy's been there for him nonetheless.

Roy looks away uncomfortably. "You don't need to thank me, brother. The truth is, I've always been jealous of you. There's nothing you can't do. You even managed to solve the case and save Maybelle. When I measure myself up to you, I am not even half the man you are."

Richard's breath catches in his throat.

It's the first time Roy ever acknowledged anything closely resembling jealously. Over the years, he suspected it, but quickly brushed it off as something else.

"It's my fault your life came to this... for that I am sorry. I'll spend the rest of it making it up to you, Richard. I know I don't deserve it, but you've been my best friend for thirty years. I won't have it any other way."

Richard's long since forgiven him. They've both done horrible things, and now it's time to put it all behind them. Lana is finally with someone who will love her the way she deserves, and Roy can have the family he's always dreamed of.

They shake hands, Richard giving Roy a genuine smile. "Water under the bridge." They laugh. "Say, did you ever end up closing the case?"

"Yeah, pretty much. Damian killed Casey to cover up his drug habits and his molestation of Maybelle." Roy lowers his voice. "It's been closed for months."

"Okay... good." Richard sips his water, eyes darting over to Beau. "And the explosion that killed the Bandidos?"

"Seems like a stray bullet caused a fire, which triggered the explosion of ammonium nitrate. We still can't figure out why Monroe left large quantities in that building... but it's fine. Forensics confirmed it."

There are several new additions to the room. Aside from Isaac, Houston, Monroe, and his family, there is the Rebel Brotherhood. They stand off in the corner making small talk with Bonnie and Karen. Most of them look nonchalant, harmless even, almost like they belong.

The clues were all there, hiding in plain sight. All he had to do was tie them together. Beau speaks quietly to Neil; their heads huddled together as they talk.

Neil's head is inclined, a show of blanket submission.

We're all intertwined. Don't worry. You'll see. Gentrification will come here as it does everywhere else. I gave Beau the torch. It's up to him to set the world on fire.

Black and white bleed into one, a mesh of gray as Richard Clayson opens his eyes and finally sees everything.

"Yeah, you missed it, brother." Roy's voice pulls him back to the present. "When you were in the hospital, Beau and his buddies rebuilt the police station, as well as the bar. Those guys know how to build. It was quite amazing after everything was done."

"I'll bet." Richard nods.

Lana calls Roy over to help with the food. Maybelle strides over to him, with Monroe in tow, both of them looking happy and healthy. "Richard." Maybelle beams and pulls him in for a tight hug. "I never got to thank you for saving my life. I appreciate everything you did. I'm glad you'll be able to stay with us a while longer."

Richard smiles. "Anytime."

"Son," Monroe says. "I misjudged you. The Bible says: Therefore, as one trespass led to condemnation for all men, so one act of right-eousness leads to justification and life for all men. Romans 5:18. I've wronged you, scorned you, and, for that, I am sorry. I let prejudice cloud my judgment... you've always been dear to my heart, Richard, the son I never had... I am sorry. Really and truly sorry."

A lump forms in his throat.

Richard knows he can never take back the past, but he can forge toward the future, and he'll be happy to forgive all those that have wronged him.

"Apology accepted," he says, swallowing thickly. "I hope I can still call you friend."

"Always." Monroe's handshake is a firm, steady grip, and he knows he means it. "I can't thank Beau enough for paying for rehab. It means the world to us."

How interesting. Richard keeps his face impassive while he takes in that information.

They depart shortly afterward, and Beau comes bouncing up to him, slightly drunk off the punch. "Do you like it?" He nuzzles against him, burying his face in his neck.

"I love it." Richard kisses his cheek.

Beau looks up at him, evergreen jewels glittering in the low lights. This man saved his life. The realization hits him low, like a punch to the stomach.

A murderer.

Mason. Gary. Enos. Casey. Avery.

By definition a serial killer. Wicked men and women, who are by no means missed by society, were slaughtered strategically.

The wrench was stolen from the auto shop. Conveniently reported, and placed at the crime scene. Paint on Beau's bike, either from the auto shop or from writing on the wall at the police station. The butcher's knife was placed at Damian's residence, with the evidence and fingerprints all over it. Neil disappearing during the fight... he must have released Damian from prison, aiding him in getting high.

They set him up to take the fall.

The worthless cunt who used me to do everything! I could kill them all! I want them all to burn, Richard!

And they did, every last one of them.

The question is, did he know Maybelle was an addict? Was Beau using her to lure Damian in, knowing that she would be his type? Or did he force her to become a drug addict and then pay for her rehabilitation because he felt guilty?

Richard glances around again, seeing the Rebel Brotherhood mingle with the cops and other family members. It dawns on him then that Beau is creating something else, something better.

A new version of Byrmonville.

Where the rejects and law enforcement work together. After rebuilding the station, Rebel Brotherhood built up a reputation for being good, and helpful in the community. It may inspire people to look the other way while they conduct business. Ammonium nitrate must have been harvested from Monroe's farm. That's how Beau knew exactly where to find them.

It's genius. It's frightening.

His fairy lover exacted his revenge, with swift malevolence, so fast and effortless nobody suspected a thing. They're all gone now.

Everyone tying them to the case. Damian must have been collateral damage. So sick and wrong, Richard feels the hairs bristle at the nap of his neck and on his arms.

Beau.

His lover, his Valkyrie.

The whore and the sheriff. Not an unfettered howl or scream erupting from his throat, but stillness, a cool grace. The ring in his back pocket weighs a ton, but Richard wouldn't have things any other way.

With the demon on his back.

And the devil in his arms.

The End

What's Next?

RECAPTURE THE SUNLIGHT

Beau Blackwell is the bane of Byrmonville... A black stain on a pure white canvas. Who knew that he would be planning his wedding day?

Richard did.

His crazy fiancé. Beau isn't even the least bit surprised, but when people start dropping dead and fingers start pointing at the Rebel brotherhood sh*** hits the fan.

Will he ever make it down the aisle?

Engaged. Betrothed. Promised. What kind of hell did he walk into?

Death and decay are all he knows.

It's time to stop pretending.

The junkie and the whore are gone.

In its place are the sheriff and the devil.

Claw of Exile (Exiled series)

Exiled.

Cursed. Abandoned. Ryu Suzuki is no stranger to these things.

For years he wandered the Outlands with nothing but his Katana to keep him safe. Kuroi Kage—Black Shadow is what they call him. A phantom Omega. He belongs nowhere. He is no one. Until a vicious disease spreading like wildfire threatens everyone he loves.

After a series of unfortunate events, the game changes. Now he's forced to go back to his long-forgotten pack, the Silvercrest Howlers.

Suddenly, he's staring at the man who ruined everything in the first place.

The Alpha that betrayed him. The White Lotus.

Micah McCorbyn.

He also happens to be his mate.

King of the Titans (Titan's series book #1)

Revenge.

Resentment. Malevolence. Desire. It wraps around him like a familiar cloak.

Like a second skin. Years of war hardened his heart into something unfathomable. For centuries he knew nothing but retribution and the ruthlessness of death and decay. His clan lost the war. They were decimated, their way of life stripped and sold to the highest bidder.

Now he finally has a chance to take back everything he lost.

To kill the King of Titans, assassin Julian White pretends to be a courtesan.

Falling in love with Lucious Rex, the man that tortured and killed his family is an unfortunate complication.

The Face of the Wicked

Yuli knows a predator when he sees one. A wide smile, pink lips pulled over rabid teeth. Ren Hirokazu. A trained assassin who answers to no one.

His stare cripples him. His rough voice unravels him. Yuli craves exactly what he shouldn't.

Not a human. An Android.

A criminal. A murderer. A monster.

The sweetest sin. Then a mysterious discovery forces Yuli to defect from the Yakuza. Hunted. Branded as a traitor there's nowhere left to hide.

Yuli must take the devil's hand. Where there's smoke, there's fire.

And Yuli is about to be consumed.

The Bully and the Vultures (Book #1 Series)

Thug.

Delinquent. It's no secret he's dangerous.

Miguel González doesn't have any memories that don't include cruel fists raining down on him. He's jumped from foster home to foster home before ending up in New Mexico, a wayward dump infested by rich snobs six months ago.

He knows what he looks like; tattooed with his hair buzz cut, lips downturned into a snarl.

Miguel doesn't belong.

He smokes, he drinks, he doesn't care for anyone or anything.

Students and teachers pass by him making faces at the stench. It's a new school year. There are a bunch of new faces, fresh and eager to learn as they navigate through high school.

Then there's him.

Javier Hernández isn't afraid. He welcomes the danger. Javier is loaded. An uppity prick who thinks he's better than everyone around him.

Only he isn't. Miguel wants to wipe that smug smirk clean off his face.

Miguel isn't good. He breaks beautiful things.

But Javier begs for it.

Years of Silence (book #1)

Silence.

It's oppressive. Ominous. It can be deafening.

Until it's obliterated by sound. Zander Wright can no longer keep his secrets at bay. They inch from the shadows ready to engulf him whole.

Hired assassins. Rigged car bombs. Someone wants him dead.

Zander knows he needs help, but he'd rather bite through his tongue than ask for it.

Luckily, it comes in form of ex-convict Vadim Oblonsky.

Dangerous. Delinquent. A ruthless ex-con that wants to carve him open with his tongue

and teeth.

And Zander might just let him.

Lust is a dangerous game.

It's sink or swim.

And Zander is about to drown.

AUTHOR'S NOTE

Thank you so much for taking the time to read my story. I know the journey for Richard and Beau is just beginning. I wrote "Weeps Indigo" three years ago. It's finally over. I can't express the sadness I feel over the last book of my boys. They've taught me so much about myself and writing. I'll be forever grateful to everyone who followed this story. I've never thought it would amount to much, just a nagging thought in my head. However, I knew I needed to get this story out. I am a self-published author, which means a lot of my work on this book has been manual. I never claimed to be the best. However, I am glad you decided to stay with this story and the sequel to come. To the true fans of this story: I appreciate you. Three years ago, I never thought I would be here, and it is because of you guys that I am.

Thank you so much for purchasing this book. If you enjoyed it, please consider leaving a review or recommending it to a friend.

Thank you again for your support!

Website: https://jkjonesauthor.ca/

Instagram: jkjonesauthor92

Lightning Source UK Ltd.
Milton Keynes UK
UKHW011310210223
417314UK00001BA/161